KV-203-275

MARNIE
MIDNIGHT
AND THE
MOON MYSTERY

LAURA ELLEN ANDERSON

Farshore

CONTENTS

MARNIE
MIDNIGHT

Farshore

First published in Great Britain in 2024 by Farshore
An imprint of HarperCollins*Publishers*
1 London Bridge Street, London SE1 9GF

farshore.co.uk

HarperCollins*Publishers*
Macken House, 39/40 Mayor Street Upper,
Dublin 1, D01 C9W8, Ireland

Text and illustrations copyright © 2024 Laura Ellen Anderson
The moral rights of the author and illustrator have been asserted.

ISBN 978 0 00 859133 5
Printed and bound in the UK using 100% renewable
electricity at CPI Group (UK) Ltd
1

A CIP catalogue record of this title is available from the British Library

All rights reserved. No part of this publication may be reproduced,
stored in a retrieval system, or transmitted, in any form or by any means,
electronic, mechanical, photocopying, recording or otherwise, without
the prior permission of the publisher and copyright owner.

Stay safe online. Any website addresses listed in this book are correct at the time
of going to print. However, Farshore is not responsible for content hosted by third
parties. Please be aware that online content can be subject to change and websites
can contain content that is unsuitable for children. We advise that all children
are supervised when using the internet.

This book contains FSC™ certified paper and other controlled
sources to ensure responsible forest management.

For more information visit: www.harpercollins.co.uk/green

MEET THE MINIBEASTS

MARNIE

Friendly, enthusiastic
and loves anything to
do with the moon!

FLOYD

Glambulous! And rather
fond of a cheese and onion
crisp crumb.

STAR

Princess of the
Seven Anthills and not
to be messed with.

CHAPTER 1

TWENTY-SEVEN GARDEN FENCES AWAY

In the little town of Thimbledown stood a big budlett tree where some teeny tiny creatures lived. And these teeny tiny creatures were going on a very BIG adventure!

The Snail Rail raced underground along the Slime Line at super speed. The bugs on board rode in colourful shell carriages, and the air was full of hums and clicks and flitters and flutters of critters of all shapes and sizes as they set off on their morning travels.

One carriage in particular was positively BUSTLING. Inside this little shell carriage sat the Midnights: a moth family who now had one less caterpillar and one more moth. For Marnie Midnight had recently transformed!

Marnie was the first of her brothers and sisters

to metamorphose from
caterpillar to moth.
She had cocooned on
a drizzly Wednesday
evening, wrapped
up snug as her body

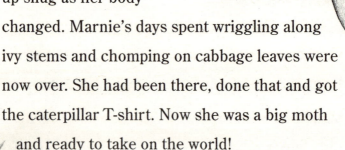

changed. Marnie's days spent wriggling along
ivy stems and chomping on cabbage leaves were
now over. She had been there, done that and got
the caterpillar T-shirt. Now she was a big moth
and ready to take on the world!

'Wiggling worm tails! I LOVE having wings!'
cried Marnie, flapping them enthusiastically
and almost knocking her little brother, Milo, out
of the carriage window.

Marnie hadn't quite got used to her new wings
yet. They were much larger than she thought
they'd be, and often got rather tangled.

Moths' wings had all sorts of different
patterns on them: Marnie's were black and grey

with curved white shapes that looked a bit like the moon. (Marnie was very happy about this because she ADORED anything to do with the moon!) She also had two fluffy feelers on her head, along with a mop of messy black hair and big orange eyes.

Today, Marnie and her brand-new wings were on a very exciting journey, accompanied by travel snacks, bubbly sap shakes and some crispy cress for Milo, who was still a squidgy little caterpillar.

Marnie's forty-eight other siblings were still tiny eggs stuck on the underside of a huge leaf at the very top of the budlett tree that was, by now, quite a few garden fences away.

'It's wonderful to see you embracing your new form, little one,' said Papa Moth, his floofy moustache hairs protruding almost as much as the hair on his slightly wonky antennae. Marvin Midnight was a wing doctor and ALWAYS wore a jumper he'd knitted, usually one with very loud designs that cheered up his patients.

'Being a moth is soooooo much better than being a caterpillar!' said Marnie with a grin, as she chomped on a bag of petal puffs. 'I don't have to live on a diet of cabbage and cress any more. Nectar is much yummier.'

'I still can't get over the fact you're off to Minibeast Academy,' said Mama Moth wiping a happy tear from her eye. Mabel Midnight was a chef at the Ruddy Carpet, their local restaurant, and always tried out the new recipes at home, much to Marnie's delight.

Her large grey-speckled wings engulfed Marnie in a warm hug. 'It feels like only yesterday you started at the Larvae Learning Zone. Look at you now – all grown up and off to BIG bug school!'

Marnie wriggled with joy. She clutched her acorn backpack, which was full to the brim with her new moon-themed stationery set and her favourite poster of Lunora Wingheart – the famous moonologist who had spent her life studying the mysteries of the ancient moths and their use of moon magic. Lunora had been a pupil at Minibeast Academy too! Marnie wanted to be just like her, and couldn't wait to follow in her flutterings.

'I can't wait to leave the budlett tree and go to big school,' whined Milo, chewing grumpily on a large mouthful of cress. 'You get to live a whole twenty-seven garden fences away from home!'

'You'll be a fully fledged moth and at Minibeast Academy before you know it,' said Marnie, before yawning the biggest and longest yawn she'd ever yawned. 'It may take a while to get used to being up this early, though.'

The sun had been rising when Marnie and her family left home that morning. During the daytime Marnie was usually fast asleep, like most moths. But she would have to get used to a different sleeping routine now she was joining Minibeast Academy. In order to make sure all the different bugs were happy – both daytime and night-time creatures – lessons started in the middle of the day and went on until the middle of the night. It meant that every minibeast could see how each other lived.

'What you need is a nice warm cup of nectar tea for energy!' said Papa Moth, holding up a steaming mug of the sweet-smelling juice, before grabbing a generous helping of petal puffs in each of his three other hands. '*And* it's very good for the thorax.'

Mama Moth sighed. 'Marvin, darling, you know it's bad manners to eat and drink from all four arms at once.'

'What's the point of having four of them then?' said Papa Moth innocently, giving Marnie a wink.

The Snail Rail continued to carry them along,

through the network of twisty underground tunnels, passing stops for Wingchester, Pond Street and Pestminster. They were now many garden fences away from their budlett tree home.

'Shouldn't be too long until we reach Minibeast Academy. Once we've passed under the city of Miniopolis, it'll be just a few stops away,' Marvin said with a grin, playfully ruffling Marnie's hair.

'What are you looking forward to most at big bug school?'

'Learning more about the moon!' Marnie said without a second thought. 'And flying practice, of course. In fact, I want to get strong enough to fly to the moon, just like Lunora Wingheart tried to do.' Marnie pulled out the rolled-up poster of Lunora Wingheart and hugged it tight.

'Why did Lunora bother flying to the moon? It's SO far away,' said Milo as he attempted to steal one of Marnie's petal puffs.

'Because, little brother of mine, she was trying to find the forgotten Book of Moon Spells,' said Marnie matter-of-factly as she moved her snacks out of Milo's reach.

'But isn't moon magic just a critter tale?' asked her brother. 'How can you find something that isn't real?'

'Well, nobody knows for sure,' replied Marnie. 'But Lunora Wingheart believed that moon magic really exists, and I do too.'

'Yeah, but look at what happened to Lunora What's-her-wing,' said Milo. 'She got EATEN by the big, scary Early Bird! Maybe you will too!' He grinned a cheeky grin. 'Then I'd be the oldest of our brothers and sisters.'

'Enough of that, thank you, Milo Midnight,' said Mama Moth sternly. 'If you don't behave, the Early Bird will come for you next,' she warned.

This usually worked when young bugs were trying their luck. (It certainly had when Marnie was a caterpillar – she'd once decorated their living-room walls with poo, and when she found out that her actions MIGHT get her an unwanted visit from the Early Bird, she never decorated anything with poo ever again.) Somehow, though, these terrifying warnings just egged Milo on even more.

'Lunora must've been REALLY naughty!' he bellowed.

Marnie rolled her eyes. 'I'm sure Lunora wasn't naughty, and we don't know if she actually got eaten,' she said with a frown. 'Lunora disappeared. But she believed that the Book of Moon Spells was still out there, and I do too! Anyway, I'll make sure I don't get eaten.'

'You probably will,' teased Milo. 'I think the Early Bird would eat your antennae for starters, and your face for dessert!'

'MILO,' Mabel snapped. Then she turned to Marvin and muttered, 'You really need to stop leaving your *True Grime* magazines out where Milo can find them.'

'Whatever happened to Lunora Wingheart, I'm sure she would have been very proud of you, my little mothling,' said Papa Moth, putting a comforting arm around his daughter.

Marnie grinned and snuggled up to her dad, taking in his musty, mothy scent.

What if all the critter tales about moon magic weren't JUST tales? Marnie thought to herself. In her heart she knew there was more to the moon than met the eye. Something . . . magical!

CHAPTER 2

FABRIC IS NOT FOOD!

As the snail rail sped under the city of Miniopolis, Marnie's mind wandered. She imagined herself meeting Lunora Wingheart. She gazed at her special poster, at Lunora's big bright yellow eyes and her beautiful moon-patterned turquoise wings. Marnie wished she could have met Lunora in real life. But for now, she'd have to pretend. Poster-Lunora looked so happy to see Marnie; it was as if this Lunora WAS real. Then Poster-Lunora reached out and —

'LOOK!' came Milo's voice, followed by a poke in the head, snapping Marnie out of her moondream. He pointed at the world outside the carriage window, where it was sparkling with daylight now that the Snail Rail had emerged from the underground.

They were just passing a large sign that read:

**YOU ARE NOW LEAVING
MINIOPOLIS
WE look forward to seeing
you again
(UNLESS YOU'RE A WASP)**

Marnie's little tummy did a big roly-poly.

'We're almost there! Oh, I hope the teachers are nice,' she said as a wave of nervousness swept through her, from her toes to the tips of her wings.

'Oh, they were grand when your mum and I were young 'uns,' said Papa Moth reassuringly.

'Young 'uns? I thought parents were born old?' Milo cut in.

'I'm curious whether Caretaker Wincy the spider is still working there after all these years,'

pondered Marvin, ignoring Milo. 'I also wonder if she still has nine legs?'

Marnie's antennae flickered in confusion. 'NINE legs? Don't spiders usually have eight legs?'

'Never ask about the ninth leg,' Papa Moth said solemnly.

The train carriage door suddenly burst open. In stepped a very tall, beige moth with straggly wings and an even stragglier face. He looked behind, then side to side.

Papa Moth raised a mug of nectar tea to the unexpected visitor. 'Can we help you?' he asked.

'Are you the snack moth?' said Milo hopefully. 'I want nectar. Mum and Dad won't let me have it.'

'Milo, how many times must we tell you, you can't have nectar until you've transformed,' Mama Moth said with a sigh.

'I've got something WAY better than nectar,' said the straggly looking moth. His voice was hoarse, and he smelled a bit like stale washing. He opened out a dishevelled wing to reveal rows and rows of what looked like tiny patches of fabric.

'I've got a sublime set of swatches here,' he said. 'Premium alpaca wool, sourced straight from the finest wardrobes!'

'Why would we want to eat that?' Milo said.

'I heard about these moths,' Marnie whispered to her brother. 'They like to eat clothes.'

'PROTEIN, my friend!' shouted the clothes moth, making Marnie jump. He opened out his other wing, revealing more rows of textured goods. 'I only offer the most keratin-rich silk. Or how about some genuine cashmere pockets? The texture is delightful.'

'Maybe we could try a little bit . . .' suggested Milo.

The straggly moth's eyes lit up.

'Milo, fabric is NOT food,'

Mama Moth said firmly.

'I'll take your finest swatch of red wool in exchange for this,' said a jovial voice.

A small, unusual-looking bee in a green leaf hat was standing in the doorway, holding out a golden silk hanky. The bee had black stripes on the top half of his yellow body, but SPOTS on his bottom half. Marnie had never seen a bee with spots on his bum, although she thought she recognised this bee's face. But how . . . ?

The moth handed over the red wool, then snatched the square of golden silk from the bee.

'We have a DEAL!' he exclaimed, before eating the hanky in one swift gulp and bustling away into the next carriage.

'This really is not my taste,' said the bee with a shudder, before wrapping the strip of red wool around his stripy shoulders. 'But it's definitely my look. I've been searching for the perfect scarf for weeks.' He gave a little bow, making the

jewels on his two antennae jingle. 'I'm Floyd Flombiddium.'

Flombiddium . . . Marnie was sure she'd heard that name before.

'Are you on your way to Minibeast Academy?' Floyd continued.

'Yes,' said Marnie with a shy wave. 'My name's Marnie Midnight. It's my first term.'

'Well, that is utterly BOMBASTIC,' said the bee. 'It's my first term too!'

Floyd sat himself down with the Midnights

and picked out a petal puff. 'Ah! My second favourite snack,' he said happily.

'What's your first favourite?' asked Marnie.

Floyd patted his satchel. 'You can't beat the crumb of a cheese and onion crisp. Father packed me a month's supply.'

'Is your dad here with you?' asked Mama Moth, looking concerned that a young bee might be travelling alone.

'Oh, he was too busy at the Higgledy Hives making his newest batch of honey.' Floyd looked a little sad, but then he smiled quickly. 'It's OK, though – I don't mind!'

'YOU'RE THE FACE OF FLOMBIDDIUM'S FAMOUS HONEY!' Marnie shrieked suddenly, making Milo curl up in surprise. 'I knew I'd seen you somewhere before!'

Floyd tipped his hat. 'Ah, yes, my face is on many jars these days.'

'Your father makes the best honey,' said Papa

Moth, looking impressed. 'I often recommend it to my patients. Helps soothe a sore bottom.'

Milo stopped chewing his cress and looked Floyd up and down. 'Speaking of bottoms . . . You're a very funny-looking bee.'

Marnie put her head in her hands.

'What?' said Milo. 'I've never seen a bee with spots on his bum before.'

'That's because I'm not quite a bee,' said Floyd. 'I'm sixty per cent bee, thirty-nine per cent ladybird, and the remaining one per cent we do not discuss. Therefore, I consider myself more of . . . an A.'

'Why?' Milo said.

'Not a Y,' corrected Floyd. 'An A.'

'I meant,' said Milo, 'why are you an A?'

Floyd flourished his new scarf. 'Well, why be a B when you can be an A?' he said. 'But on bad days I make myself an F. Those are dark days . . . although sometimes it's only because I've just not realised it's night-time!'

Just then, Papa Moth pointed out of the window. 'Take a look at that, kids!' he cried.

Towering above them, creating long shadows in the morning light, was the most gargantuan building Marnie had ever seen. She leaned so far out of the carriage she was almost swept away in the breeze.

'Wow!' she gasped. 'What's that?'

'That, my dear Marnie, is the Museum of Nature,' Papa Moth said. 'Minibeast Academy was built in the museum gardens centuries ago, back when the mighty earwig Saint Helena was still around.' He bowed his head. 'May she rest in pieces.'

Marine could make out a few strange-shaped silhouettes in the tall windows of the museum. Her wings flickered nervously. Those shapes were definitely not bugs!

CHAPTER 3

LOTS OF MASSIVE BITS

'Are those actual Swatters?' Marnie whispered. She'd heard about them but had never seen a Swatter in real life before.

'Don't worry,' Mama Moth reassured her. 'You're safe from any stray ones, as long as you stay within the school grounds.'

'Until your last year,' added Papa Moth. 'Then you spend half a term among the Swatters. For work experience.'

Marnie's wings gave a nervous twitch, slapping Floyd on the back and causing him to cough up a petal puff.

'Marvin, dear!' hissed Mabel. 'Marnie doesn't have to think about that for a long time yet.' She rubbed the back of Marnie's wings comfortingly.

'My family call them the Screamers,' said Floyd, nodding at the silhouettes. 'They see us

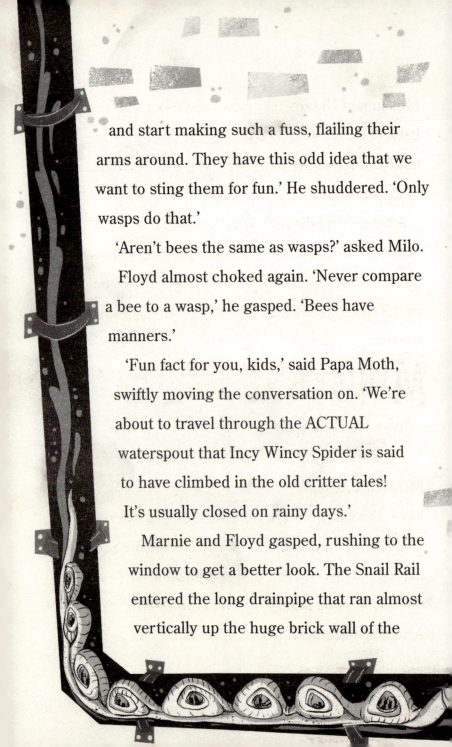

and start making such a fuss, flailing their arms around. They have this odd idea that we want to sting them for fun.' He shuddered. 'Only wasps do that.'

'Aren't bees the same as wasps?' asked Milo.

Floyd almost choked again. 'Never compare a bee to a wasp,' he gasped. 'Bees have manners.'

'Fun fact for you, kids,' said Papa Moth, swiftly moving the conversation on. 'We're about to travel through the ACTUAL waterspout that Incy Wincy Spider is said to have climbed in the old critter tales! It's usually closed on rainy days.'

Marnie and Floyd gasped, rushing to the window to get a better look. The Snail Rail entered the long drainpipe that ran almost vertically up the huge brick wall of the

Museum of Nature, along the guttering and back to the ground again. They were now on their last leg of the journey, in the back gardens of the museum.

After driving through what seemed like miles of tall green grass, the Snail Rail gradually slowed down, before finally stopping beside a long tree root. Carved into the root platform were the words:

MiNiBEAST ACADEMY

'We're here!' Papa Moth cried happily.

Marnie gulped. She'd been SO excited to start Minibeast Academy, but now she was actually here, she was getting fluttery feelings in her toes!

As the Midnight family stepped out of the shell carriage, Floyd twirled one antenna and said quietly, 'Do you mind if we walk into Minibeast Academy together?'

Marnie smiled at him. She sensed he was feeling just as nervous as her. 'Of course!' she said.

Linking arms with Floyd, she immediately felt so much better. It was lovely to already have a friend!

Floyd let out a relieved sigh. 'I fear I might shed five to ten tears of happiness, but that would make my face all puffy – and you don't want to see my puffy face. It looks like a beetle's bottom.'

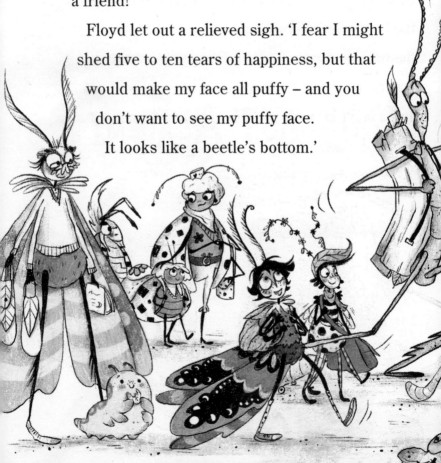

Marnie found herself in fits of giggles. It was impossible not to smile around Floyd Flombiddium!

Other young bugs starting school were also leaving the Snail Rail with their families. A teeny-tiny ant with a HUGE backpack marched along confidently. A tall stick insect stepped right over the heads of the crowd and lolloped through the bustling bugs. A nervous-looking centipede scurried past a trio of moody-looking mosquitos, and a ladybird with squares instead of spots plodded along.

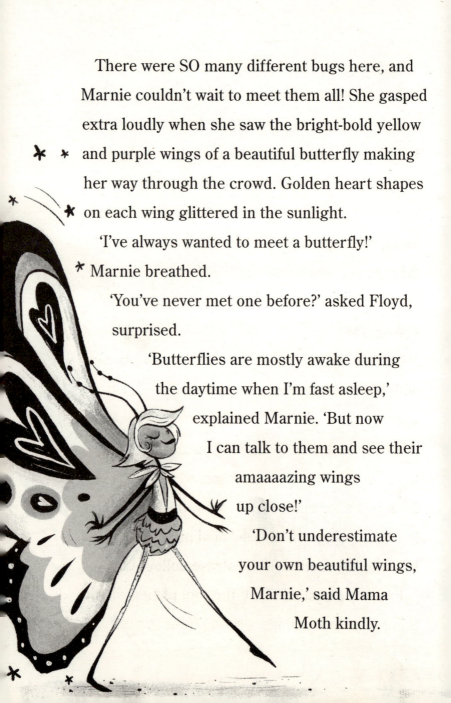

There were SO many different bugs here, and Marnie couldn't wait to meet them all! She gasped extra loudly when she saw the bright-bold yellow and purple wings of a beautiful butterfly making her way through the crowd. Golden heart shapes on each wing glittered in the sunlight.

'I've always wanted to meet a butterfly!' Marnie breathed.

'You've never met one before?' asked Floyd, surprised.

'Butterflies are mostly awake during the daytime when I'm fast asleep,' explained Marnie. 'But now I can talk to them and see their amaaaazing wings up close!'

'Don't underestimate your own beautiful wings, Marnie,' said Mama Moth kindly.

Marnie smiled at her mum as she tried to spot the butterfly in the crowd again. She loved her own new wings, but she knew they'd never be as bright and colourful as a butterfly's!

'Attention, first-year bugs!' called out an efficient-looking firefly in a bow tie. His abdomen suddenly erupted with a yellowy-green light. 'My name is Squire-fly Fred. I am a fourth-year student at Minibeast Academy and I will be your guide.'

Marnie felt her wings flicker faster and faster with nervous excitement, causing Floyd's hat to waft off his head.

'Feel free to ask me any questions you might have over the next few days and nights . . . apart from just after dinner,' continued the firefly. 'That is when I carry out my essential nightly belly-brightening routine. Now, please, follow me.'

Everyone bustled along the root platform after Squire-fly Fred and his glowing tummy. Soon

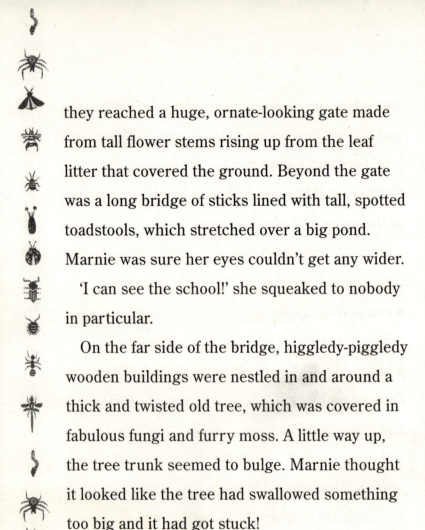

they reached a huge, ornate-looking gate made from tall flower stems rising up from the leaf litter that covered the ground. Beyond the gate was a long bridge of sticks lined with tall, spotted toadstools, which stretched over a big pond. Marnie was sure her eyes couldn't get any wider.

'I can see the school!' she squeaked to nobody in particular.

On the far side of the bridge, higgledy-piggledy wooden buildings were nestled in and around a thick and twisted old tree, which was covered in fabulous fungi and furry moss. A little way up, the tree trunk seemed to bulge. Marnie thought it looked like the tree had swallowed something too big and it had got stuck!

Huts made from sticks disappeared way up into the leaves, while mushrooms protruded from the main trunk at all angles, alongside hanging pods and hollow stems. The pond ran around the tree's large roots like a moat. Tangled bushes and vibrant flower beds surrounded the bustling bug dwelling, hiding it from the eyes of the Swatters and Screamers in the gigantic museum at the other end of the garden.

It was Minibeast Academy!

'Come on!' cried Marnie, speeding up into a run across the bridge.

Floyd just about kept up, his antennae jingling, until Marnie skidded to a halt at the flowery archway that was the school's entrance, and Floyd face-planted on the floor beside her.

'I don't think I'm designed for running,' he puffed. 'That's why I have wings.'

'And THIS is where we'll learn to use them properly!' said Marnie cheerfully, pointing up at the school.

Mama Moth's lip wobbled as she caught up with them.

'Muuuum, you said you wouldn't cry,' said Marnie, doing her best to smile, although her tummy gave a nervous little twist.

Mama Moth sniffed. 'I'm allowed to cry. I'm your mother. Here, I made you a list . . .' She delved into her handbag. Mama Moth loved a list. Sometimes she even listed the lists she needed to . . . list!

'I've made a note of all your important contacts, including the local doc-moth, the emergency earwigs and, of course, our World Wide Web code,' said Mama Moth, handing her daughter a bundle of eucalyptus scrolls. 'There's also a list of special dates to remember . . .'

'Including MY Transformation Day!' added Milo loudly, clearly feeling a bit left out.

'Thanks, Mum!' said Marnie, tucking the scrolls into her already full backpack.

'And I hand-made you a little something,' said Papa Moth. From under his wing, he took out the

most beautiful jumper. It was a vibrant red, with
a silvery moon woven on to its front. 'It's got
holes in all the right places,' he said proudly.

'I love it!' Marnie squealed, throwing her arms
around her dad.

Papa Moth pulled the jumper gently over
Marnie's head and untucked her wings. It
fitted perfectly.

'Just don't wear it whenever you visit Aunt Helen,' he added. 'She recently married a clothes moth and, well, you'll end up with holes in all the *wrong* places.'

Marnie's parents wrapped their wings around her, and Milo joined in reluctantly.

'I hate hugs,' he mumbled.

'How can you hate hugs?' said Floyd, who was standing nearby. 'They're one of the best things ever.'

Marnie poked her head out from between her mum and dad's wings and then grabbed the bee-who-was-actually-an-A and pulled him into the Midnight family embrace. 'Hugs are for everyone!'

Squire-Fly Fred's tummy light began to flash. Pulsating from yellow to green, blue, purple and fluorescent pink, it resembled a mini disco ball.

'First years!' he bellowed. 'Time to go!'

Marnie took a deep breath. 'I'll miss you all,'

she said, putting on a brave face. It helped having her new friend Floyd by her side.

'Whenever you're missing home, just look at the moon,' said Papa Moth gently. 'And know that the moon you see is the same moon we can see. Even though we're many garden fences away from each other, the moon shines on us all, connecting us.'

'That's a really nice way of thinking about it,' said Floyd, smiling.

'The moon will always help me to feel brave,' said Marnie, clutching her backpack.

Just before his sister walked away, Milo wriggled up to Marnie. 'I won't miss you one little bit . . .' he said to her, then he gave her a cheeky, cress-filled grin. 'I'll miss you LOTS OF MASSIVE BITS!'

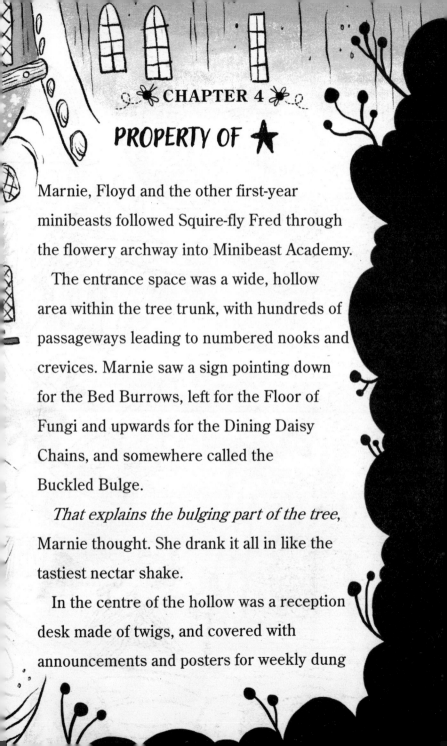

CHAPTER 4

PROPERTY OF ⭐

Marnie, Floyd and the other first-year minibeasts followed Squire-fly Fred through the flowery archway into Minibeast Academy.

The entrance space was a wide, hollow area within the tree trunk, with hundreds of passageways leading to numbered nooks and crevices. Marnie saw a sign pointing down for the Bed Burrows, left for the Floor of Fungi and upwards for the Dining Daisy Chains, and somewhere called the Buckled Bulge.

That explains the bulging part of the tree, Marnie thought. She drank it all in like the tastiest nectar shake.

In the centre of the hollow was a reception desk made of twigs, and covered with announcements and posters for weekly dung

deliveries, a Wriggle or Wiggle? debate,
Invertebration Day and an annual Great
Critter Contest.

'Leave your bags with Caretaker Wincy,
who will make sure they're taken to your Bed
Burrows,' called Squire-fly Fred.

Marnie peered at the incredibly old spider
behind the reception desk. She looked as if she'd
shrivelled up and come back to life again.

'She's the one!' Marnie whispered.

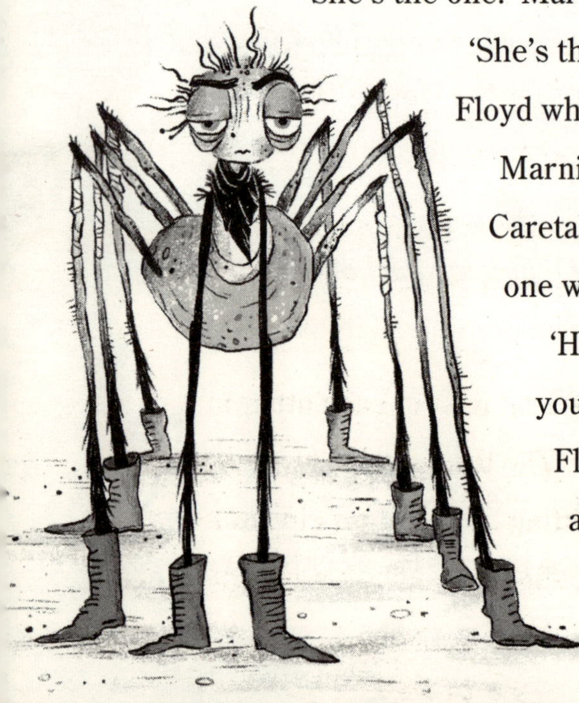

'She's the one, what?'
Floyd whispered back.

Marnie nodded towards
Caretaker Wincy. 'The
one with the ninth leg!'

'Holy honeycombs,
you're right!' said
Floyd, studying the
ancient arachnid.

'How –'

'Dad said we must never ask about the ninth leg,' Marnie cut in quickly.

Floyd saluted. 'Noted!'

The group of excitable first years followed Squire-fly Fred up a wiggly staircase lining the thick tree trunk. After quite a lot of steps and even more complaining from Floyd, the bugs arrived at the entrance to an enormous dome lined with bright green moss.

'This is the Buckled Bulge where all assemblies will take place!' bellowed Squire-fly Fred, his belly still flashing different colours. 'First years, please take your seats in the front two rows. I must return to my Bioluminescence Balance lesson. Enjoy your first day at Minibeast Academy!'

Marnie and Floyd sat next to each other in the very front row. The three serious-looking mosquitos were sitting on the other side of Floyd, and a teeny ant holding a notebook was next to Marnie. It was the same ant with the massive backpack that Marnie had seen on the Snail Rail platform.

The ant sat bolt upright, looking like she didn't want to be spoken to. Marnie decided to try to make friends anyway.

'Hi, I'm Marnie Midnight!' she said brightly. 'What's your name?'

The ant gave Marnie a long, hard stare. Marnie blinked. She hadn't accidentally said something rude, had she?

The ant turned her notepad towards Marnie. Scribbled across the front cover were the words: Property of ★. There was no sign of a name.

'OK . . .' said Marnie. 'It's nice to meet you. Um, are you excited to start Minibeast Academy?'

The ant kept staring at Marnie in silence.

'Well, it's been lovely talking to you,' said Marnie, slowly turning away. She could still feel

the ant's beady eyes on her.

'I see you've met Star Vonstrosity,' Floyd
whispered.

'OH!' Marnie turned back to the ant. 'Your
notebook says Property of Star . . . but it's an
actual star. That's so cute!'

Star didn't respond.

'There is nothing cute about Star Vonstrosity,'
Floyd muttered. 'She's from the Vonstrosity

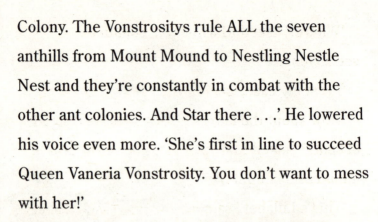

Colony. The Vonstrositys rule ALL the seven anthills from Mount Mound to Nestling Nestle Nest and they're constantly in combat with the other ant colonies. And Star there . . .' He lowered his voice even more. 'She's first in line to succeed Queen Vaneria Vonstrosity. You don't want to mess with her!'

Marnie wasn't entirely sure how to respond to that information. She could still feel Star's gaze burning into her.

Floyd nodded at the three morose mosquitos next to him. 'These guys are Marabella, Morbidilla and Melanchollia. Also known as the Tragic Triplets.'

The mosquitos looked solemnly at their own feet. Marnie just wanted to give them all a hug to cheer them up.

'And that's Meggitt the stick insect – he always gets lost,' Floyd said, nodding further along the row.

'Where?' asked Marnie. She couldn't see anyone.

'I rest my case,' said Floyd.

'How about the ladybird with squares instead of spots?' asked Marnie, gesturing to the row of minibeasts behind them.

'That's Lillabet,' said Floyd. 'And that's Gilbert Gubble,' he added, pointing to the worm beside Lillabet. 'He's so clumsy he accidently got his tail chopped off seven times . . .'

'Ouch!' cried Marnie.

'Oh, it's all right,' said Floyd dismissively, waving a hand. 'Worms' tails grow back.' He smiled. 'Oh, and then there's dear Ron.'

'What kind of bug is Ron?' asked Marnie as the six-legged, three-winged, bobbly Ron attempted to chew his fourth foot.

'Nobody knows what Ron is,' said Floyd.

There was a sudden giggle and a squeal from three butterflies sitting at the very end of the

second row. Marnie looked wistfully at them.
She wished her wings were as bright as theirs.
Especially the butterfly in the middle, whose
wings were yellow and purple with gold-heart
patterns that glittered in the sunlight peeping
through the walls of the Buckled Bulge.

'They're beautiful!' said Marnie.

'Ah, yes. The Betterflies.' Floyd raised an
eyebrow at the three giggling bugs. 'That's what
they call themselves anyway. That's Veronica
Spottage in the middle. But she tells everyone
her name is pronounced Spottarshay.' He rolled
his eyes. 'Her pals Thelma and Louise never
leave her side.'

Marnie looked curiously at Floyd. 'How do you
know about everyone already?'

Floyd flicked his new red scarf. 'I just know
things,' he said. He winked. 'That's a fancy way
of saying I'm very nosy.'

'FIRST YEARS!' a voice bellowed from above.

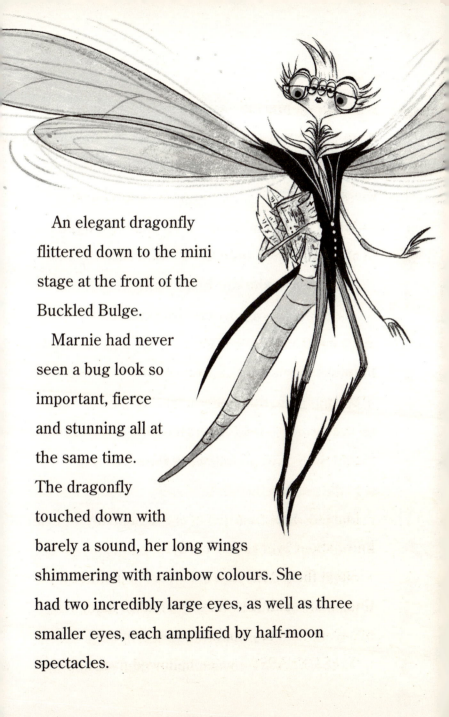

An elegant dragonfly
flittered down to the mini
stage at the front of the
Buckled Bulge.

Marnie had never
seen a bug look so
important, fierce
and stunning all at
the same time.
The dragonfly
touched down with
barely a sound, her long wings
shimmering with rainbow colours. She
had two incredibly large eyes, as well as three
smaller eyes, each amplified by half-moon
spectacles.

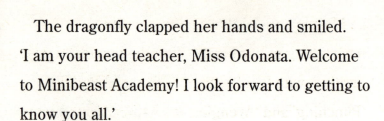

The dragonfly clapped her hands and smiled. 'I am your head teacher, Miss Odonata. Welcome to Minibeast Academy! I look forward to getting to know you all.'

'Miss Odonata was one of the best sky fighters of all time,' Floyd whispered. 'Won Best Aquatic Predator when she was just a nymph, and then two hundred and eleven Dragonfly Duels in a row as an adult before finally getting beaten by Zimmatronian Flumplesquirt.'

Marnie gulped. She definitely didn't want to get on the wrong side of Miss Odonata!

'ALL bugs will be following the same time schedule at Minibeast Academy,' the head teacher explained. 'The first half of the school day will run during the Light Hours between noon and sunset. You will then have your lunch break before the remainder of your lessons during the Dark Hours, followed by dinner and free time. All bugs MUST be in their bed burrows no later than midnight.'

Marnie noticed that Star was writing everything in her notebook in the teeniest-tiniest writing, with 'Leaf Lifting', 'Advanced Puddle Punching' and 'Avenging my Father' slotted into the margins.

'And now it's time to meet your form tutor, Mr Atlas,' said Miss Odonata.

She beckoned to a tall, miserable-looking moth with tired-looking yellow eyes. He was wearing a long grey cloak over his wings and wore an expression of annoyance.

'I heard about Mr Atlas from my big sister,' Marnie heard one of the Betterflies whisper loudly. 'He's the meanest teacher in school.'

'I've heard he gets meaner EVERY year!' added another Betterfly.

Marnie hoped they were wrong and that Mr Atlas was just saving his smiles for later.

'Your first session of the school day will always be with Mr Atlas in the Lower Roots of the

school,' Miss Odonata continued. 'He will take the register, answer any questions you have, and teach you General Bug Studies before you head off to the rest of your specialised lessons. As your form tutor, Mr Atlas will offer support and guidance throughout your time here at Minibeast Academy.'

'I'm also the first-year Predator Studies teacher,' added the grumpy-looking moth.

'So I'll be seeing more of you than I'd like.'

'Is that meant to sound supportive?' Floyd whispered.

'Before I finish and pass you all over to Mr Atlas for registration, there is something very important I must share with you,' Miss Odonata announced.

Marnie spotted a flicker of worry in the dragonfly's eyes.

'Students must NEVER go beyond the pond perimeter of the grounds without permission. As some of you may know, for many years now, a ferocious Early Bird has circled the skies looking for victims, and it is at its most active during these warmer months. The Early Bird always catches the worm . . . and plenty of other minibeasts too! Even YOU.'

The first years jumped and Floyd clutched at the pearls he was wearing under his scarf.

'If at ANY point you hear the alarm telling us that the Early Bird has been spotted, you must stay inside,' Miss Odonata said firmly. There was an awkward silence before she smiled and said, 'Enjoy your first day!'

After taking the register, Mr Atlas handed each of the first years a map of the school and their timetable of lessons. Marnie gasped when she saw the map. The school looked like a maze, with an intricate warren of passageways running up, around and through the tree bark.

'Does anyone have any questions?' he asked.

Marnie's hand shot straight up. 'Um, excuse me, sir, hello! It's nice to meet you. I'm Marnie Midnight,' she said, smiling at the old moth. 'I've been so excited to start Minibeast Academy. I want to be a Moonologist just like the great Lunora Wingheart.' She noticed Mr Atlas's eye begin to twitch. When he said nothing, Marnie continued enthusiastically. 'Will we get to learn about the moon this year?'

The teacher frowned deeply. 'There will be no talk of the moon in this school,' he said sternly. Then, with a swoosh of his cloak, he strode away.

Marnie felt very confused. Why wasn't she allowed to talk about the moon? What was going on?

CHAPTER 5
WE ARE LOST SOULS

'Lunora Wingheart learned all about the moon RIGHT HERE in this school,' Marnie spluttered crossly, as she and Floyd weaved their way through the passageways to their first lesson. 'We can't just ignore the moon! Learning all about it is what inspired Lunora to become one of the greatest moonologists and research forgotten moon magic.'

'Hmmm, it does seem strange . . .' said Floyd, tilting his head to one side and making his antennae jewels jingle. 'I've always heard stories about moon magic, but I thought they were just critter tales, a bit like the story of Incy Wincy Spider climbing up the waterspout.'

'But what if they aren't just stories?' said Marnie, her eyes wide and wild. 'What if the critter tales – like Incy Wincy and like moon magic – are real? They just happened such a long time ago that everyone has forgotten?'

Floyd gasped. 'You're saying Incy Wincy could be REAL?!' He wiggled his antennae in disbelief. 'That would be awesome! But HOW did Incy climb all the way up that spout?! I need to know!'

'Well, no one's stopping you from finding out,' Marnie said with a wink.

Marnie and the other first years sat inside Crevice Nine, a round classroom full of dappled sunshine and pictures of famous Minibeast Academy alumni. Marnie was surprised not to see a picture of Lunora Wingheart, but even more surprised to see a picture of Mystic Moth, who claimed she could see the future with her third antenna. (She could not.)

'Good day, first years! Welcome to your first official Bug History lesson. My name is Madame Figganory, and I'll be teaching you all you need to know about our past!' the ladybug teacher trilled happily, her spotty wings swooshing everybody's leaf papers from their desks. 'But before we crack on, I'd love to get to know each of you a little more. Why don't you tell us about a bug from the past who has inspired YOU!'

Madame Figganory checked her register and smiled. 'Why don't we have the mosquito triplets first? Marabella, Morbidilla and Melanchollia . . .' She said, gesturing to the trio of miserable-looking insects.

The trio stood up. Melanchollia spoke first in a flat voice. 'We were inspired by Vlad the Bloodsucker. But we recently found out we can't drink blood any more.'

'It gives us a rash,' Morbidilla continued.

'Without blood, we are lost souls and will probably become extinct,' finished Marabella.

The class was silent, apart from one rather inconveniently timed fart from the back of the room.

'Oh . . . well, that's very . . . unfortunate,' said Madame Figganory, looking a little lost for words.

Marnie put her hand up, but the teacher had turned her attention to Star.

'How about YOU, Miss Vonstrosity?'

Star stood up straight. 'There is no inspiration, only vengeance,' she said, before sitting back down.

Madame Figganory's smile began to look a little strained. 'Does . . . anyone have anything to share that doesn't involve extinction and revenge . . . ?'

Marnie put her hand up even higher.

'Go on, Marnie Midnight – you look like you're bursting to share!'

Marnie stood up and shook her wings, knocking her

pencil case on to the floor. She cleared
her throat.

'My biggest inspiration is Lunora Wingheart.
She was a great moonologist – that's someone
who studies everything about the moon – and
she went to THIS school! I want to be just like
her when I grow up.'

'Well, that is interesting, Marnie!' Madame
Figganory smiled, looking relieved. 'Do tell us
more about Lunora Wingheart.'

Marnie grinned. She loved talking about
Lunora Wingheart, and it was so exciting to
be sharing her love for Lunora with the new
bugs in class.

'Lunora was fascinated by the stories of the
ancient moths. Once a month, when the moon
was full, moths from all around the world would
fly to the moon to meet each other and share
new spells to add to their Book of Moon Spells,'
she said, shivering with excitement.

There was a snigger from the back of the classroom where the Betterflies were sitting.

'I love the sound of this moon magic. How does it work?' Floyd winked at Marnie and she felt a warmth rise inside her.

'The moths needed moonlight to cast their spells,' Marnie continued. The book contained all their spells, written down over hundreds of years.'

'Well . . . you have quite the imagination, Marnie!' said Madame Figganory, looking slightly baffled. 'What a fun story!'

'Oh, it's not just a story, miss,' Marnie said.

Before the teacher could reply, Star put her hand up and asked Marnie seriously, 'Could these moths use the magic to explode stuff?'

Marnie grinned – Star was speaking to her at last!

'Nobody knows,' said Marnie, 'because the Book of Moon Spells hasn't been seen for centuries. As more lights filled the Earth, the moths' visits to the moon became less frequent, and slowly moon magic was forgotten. Now, it's all seen as one big critter tale.'

'That's because it IS a critter tale,' Veronica scoffed, her bright wings flickering meanly.

'Well, Lunora didn't think so,' Marnie replied. 'Lunora believed so deeply in moon magic that she embarked on a mission to fly to the moon in the hope of finding the long lost Book of Moon Spells. But sadly she disappear–'

'There's no such thing as magic!' interrupted Veronica. 'And why would this book be kept on the moon?'

Marnie shook her head. 'That's the way it had always been,' she said. 'The ancient moths kept moon magic all to themselves. But I'm going to change that! I believe moon magic is for everyone!'

Veronica burst out laughing. 'I have never

heard anything so ridiculous,' she said spitefully.

'Well, you don't have to believe it,' said Marnie, feeling upset at the way the butterfly was behaving. 'But I do. My wings tingle in the moonlight, and I just *know* there's something more to our wonderful moon. If we could find the Book of Moon Spells, we could learn all about it. And that means going to the moon!'

'Eurgh! Imagine wasting your time searching for something that's not even there! Pathetic.' Veronica rolled her eyes and blew a raspberry.

'RIGHT. I think that's enough for today,' Madame Figganory said firmly as Marnie glared at Veronica. 'Let's get this lesson started!'

Their first Bug History lesson was spent studying the one-hundred-year Battle for the Spotted Throne, which had recently been adapted into a live show called *Ladybird, Ladybird, Fly Away Home!* starring McLady Rouge.

Next was Flying Practice, where Marnie and

Floyd partnered up. The whole lesson was spent learning how to hover in the air for two minutes (Floyd ended up upside down and Marnie's wings kept getting in a terrible tangle, but they had fun), while the minibeasts without wings attended Stomper Dodging.

Just when Marnie thought her wings might fall off from tiredness, it was time for Critter Calculus.

While Marnie unsuccessfully tried to solve the parametric equation for a rose's petal, she felt her wings tingling. As her mind began to wander she seemed to find herself on the moon with Lunora Wingheart. The great moonologist was reaching out to her and saying something that sounded like 'Help m–'

All of a sudden Marnie was literally snapped out of her moondream by the school snapdragon screeching 'SNAAAAAAAP' three times to announce lunch break. For such a pretty flower, it made a very horrible noise.

Marnie blinked a few times. She had always been a moondreamer, but she had never had a moondream about Lunora Wingheart that had felt quite so REAL before . . .

CHAPTER 6
NAUGHTY NIGEL

Marnie hadn't realised how hungry she was until she approached the Dining Daisy Chains for lunch. The sun was setting as young minibeasts of all shapes and sizes sat on the white petals that surrounded the large yellow discs. The whole place was full of munching and slurping and sipping and burping. It was a feast for ALL the senses!

There were lots of nectar-filled goods for the insects to eat, as well as decaying foods for those with more specialised tastes. Marnie and Floyd helped themselves to a nice big bowl of nectar noodles each.

As they munched, Marnie spotted Veronica gliding perfectly towards a petal seat, fluttering her wings and flicking her curly antennae. Marnie still felt upset about the butterfly's mean comments in class.

'How can she fly so well already?' said Floyd, following Marnie's gaze. 'I can just about achieve a few flutters between walking. We should give that a name . . . Flawking? Wuttering?'

Marnie sighed. 'I was really hoping to make friends with a butterfly.'

'Don't let what Veronica said bother you,' said Floyd softly. Then he gasped and bellowed, 'FLUTTALKING. That works, right?'

'Maybe I just need to try again?' Marnie said, sitting up a little straighter.

'The fluttalking or the Veronica-ing?' asked Floyd.

'Veronica . . .' Marnie replied, thinking hard. 'Sometimes bugs react strangely to things they don't understand. It happens a lot when I talk about moon magic.'

Floyd grimaced. 'Maybe – although I don't think those so-called Betterflies are very nice minibeasts!'

Once they'd finished eating, the two friends decided to explore the school before the next lot of lessons began.

Marnie and Floyd fluttalked up through the main trunk, taking a left along one of the branch passages. They passed the Wall of Weeds, with Floyd naming them all.

'I do love a dancing dandelion, although I've never agreed with their weed status,' he said as they passed the yellow blooms jigging from side to side. 'Not so keen on the creeping caroline, though . . . and there's the shepherd's backpack – particularly good for buttock boils . . . Ah, here's the lesser-known naughty nigel.' He pointed to a weed that resembled tall top hats perched upon stems.

'What does the naughty nigel do?' asked Marnie.

Floyd shook his head. 'Oh, it's far too naughty to tell.'

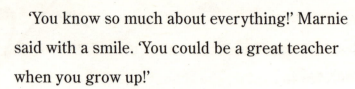

'You know so much about everything!' Marnie said with a smile. 'You could be a great teacher when you grow up!'

'Well, as I said before, I'm just very nosy.' Floyd chuckled. 'I love learning about LOTS of different things, but mostly from listening or looking at pictures. I've never been very good at reading words.' He flicked his scarf dramatically. 'When I grow up, I really want to be an artist and to paint the finest nectar portraits of bugs from around the world!'

'Wow!' said Marnie. 'That sounds like the best job!'

As the two friends made their way further along the branch past more crevices, Marnie checked her map.

'Oooh, we're at the Hive Hollows!' she said, admiring a row of yellow hexagonal spaces stretching out before them. In one of the classrooms, she saw a bee professor move around in sequential motions, wiggling and shaking her bottom, while the bee students watched and took notes.

'Ooo! That must be the lunchtime Waggle Club!' said Floyd.

'Waggle Club?' Marnie repeated. 'Is that some kind of bee dance?'

'It's like secret bee code!' Floyd proclaimed. 'We can talk to each other without saying anything.'

'How do you know what they're saying?' Marnie asked. 'The teacher just looks as if she's got fairyflies in her pants!'

'Oh, no,' said Floyd. 'She's quoting the famous poem "The Pedigree of Honey" by Emily Dickinson.'

'You got that from a wiggle?!' asked Marnie in amazement.

'A waggle,' Floyd corrected her.

'Please can you teach me the secret waggle

code!' cried Marnie.

Floyd turned his head from side to side, flickered his wings twice and clasped two hands together. 'Bees do this to let other bees know they're OK on long journeys.'

Marnie tried to copy Floyd, turning her head from side to side. She flapped her wings a bit too hard, tripped over and ended up doing a backwards roly-poly.

'Did that mean anything at all?' asked Marnie, giggling as she clambered to her feet.

'I do believe you were trying to ask for the eyelid

of a tangerine . . .' Floyd said with a snort of laughter.

Flutter-walking even further up the school (past the Pollen Packing and Stinger Safety crevices), Marnie and Floyd soon found themselves in a part of the school that was dark and eerily quiet.

'Feels like this area is a bit neglected,' said Marnie curiously as she approached a passageway that wound upwards into complete darkness.

'What's up there?' asked Floyd.

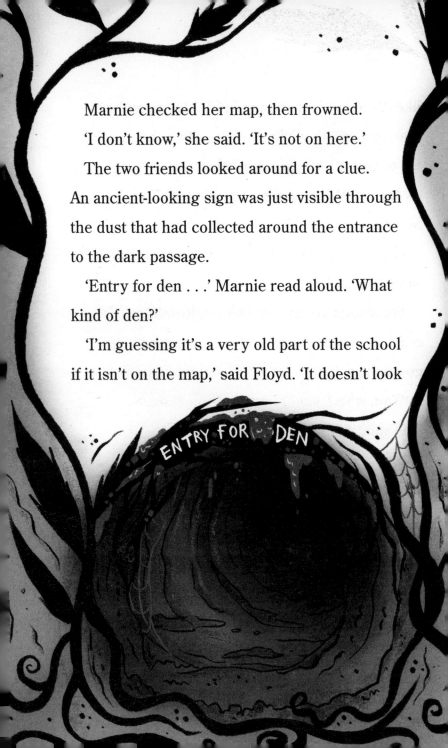

Marnie checked her map, then frowned.

'I don't know,' she said. 'It's not on here.'

The two friends looked around for a clue.
An ancient-looking sign was just visible through
the dust that had collected around the entrance
to the dark passage.

'Entry for den . . .' Marnie read aloud. 'What
kind of den?'

'I'm guessing it's a very old part of the school
if it isn't on the map,' said Floyd. 'It doesn't look

like it's been cleaned in a VERY long time. Either that, or Caretaker Wincy needs to put her ninth leg to better use.'

'Are you thinking what I'm thinking?' said Marnie.

They both grinned before both speaking at the same time.

'We should go up there and explore!' Marnie cried as Floyd declared, 'We should never, ever go up there!'

'Wait, what?' said Floyd in astonishment. 'You want to explore? Doesn't it give you the heebie-beejies?! No, wait, I mean, the beebie-jeebies . . . Hold on . . . Oh, never mind.'

'I want to check it out!' said Marnie excitedly. There was something about this place that was making her wings tingle.

'Hmm, I'm not sure . . .' said Floyd in a worried tone of voice. 'Perhaps we can explore somewhere a little less creepy?' He looked at the map. 'The Floor of Fungi sounds fun!'

'All righty then,' said Marnie. 'I'll meet you on the Floor of Fungi after I've checked out this spooOOOooky den!' She took one step into the stairwell. Then another.

'Eurgh, fine,' said Floyd, following behind. 'I'm just too nosy for my own good.'

Marnie was secretly relieved to have Floyd with her as she entered the passageway. It was incredibly steep and very dark, although luckily Marnie's large moth eyes meant she found it quite easy to see as they climbed. After all, moths LOVED the night-time, and back home Marnie used to explore with only the silvery light of the moon to guide her.

Floyd wasn't having such an easy time of it, so Marnie held one of his hands so that she could steer him.

After winding around for what felt like forever,

to have actually met you. You're my biggest inspiration.' She looked up at the old moth, happy tears filling her eyes. 'I've always wanted to follow in your flutterings. Thank you for never giving up on moon magic.'

Lunora smiled. 'Thank YOU, Marnie Midnight, for never giving up on me.'

CHAPTER 7

NOPE, NOPETY, NOPE

'Moon Club!' cried Marnie, running over to the dusty door. 'So they DO learn about the moon here!'

'Or rather, they did . . .' Floyd waltzed over and drew a heart shape in the thick grime coating the window in the door. 'It all looks a bit old and forgotten.'

Marnie pressed her face up against the window, peering through Floyd's heart. But it was still too dirty to see anything.

'Lunora Wingheart might have STOOD IN THIS VERY CLASSROOM,' squealed Marnie. 'Let's have a quick peek inside.' She grabbed the grubby handle, but the door didn't budge.

Then something caught her eye. She gasped and a shiver ran down her spine.

'What?' cried Floyd. 'Is there dirt on my hat?!'

'I'm SURE I saw something move,' Marnie replied.

Something dark zipped across their line of sight, making Marnie jump and Floyd scramble backwards in alarm.

'NOPE, NOPETY, NOPE,' he said firmly. 'This is WAY too creepy for our first day at school. This is the kind of thing that happens at least halfway through the first year . . . We've barely finished our first lunch break!'

Marnie's little heart was pounding.

Floyd shuddered. 'You don't think it's a ghost-bug, do you?' he whispered loudly. 'Perhaps that's why they stopped the Moon Studies lessons. Maybe the classroom was haunted!'

There was a cough behind them and a small shape emerged through the darkness.

'GHOST-BUUUUUUG!' shrieked Floyd, and the two minibeasts almost jumped right out of

their exoskeletons. Floyd covered his face with his scarf before whispering dramatically, 'Is it over? Am I dead?'

'Not yet,' said a stern voice. 'But death comes for us all eventually.'

'Star?!' said Marnie, clutching her thumping chest. 'You scared the antennae off us!'

Floyd lowered his scarf. 'Why must she be so terrifying?' he whispered to Marnie.

'As well as being terrifying,' said Star, 'I was also born with advanced acoustic receptors that respond to the tiniest sound particle velocity.'

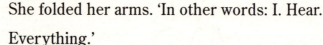

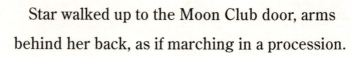

She folded her arms. 'In other words: I. Hear. Everything.'

Marnie gulped.

Star walked up to the Moon Club door, arms behind her back, as if marching in a procession.

'I wouldn't go near that if I were you,' said Floyd.

But Star poked the door once, before pressing her face up against it.

She began to frown. The frown grew deeper and deeper, and then there was a BUMP before the door handle began to creak.

Marnie didn't even have time to scream. Before she realised what she was doing, she was pelting back along the dark winding passage, dragging Floyd and Star along with her.

A moment later, the three bugs found themselves at the base of the passage, rather more dusty and grimy than they'd been before. Marnie spotted an empty nook labelled 'STORE CUPBOARD' just big enough for the three bugs and pulled them into it.

When she finally caught her breath, she said, 'What was in that room?'

'Well, whatever it is, it can stay there,' said Floyd. 'Because I am never going up there ever again.'

'It's forbidden anyway,' Star said calmly.

'What's forbidden?' said Floyd, looking utterly confused.

Star rolled her eyes. 'Entry to whatever's up there is forbidden.'

'But it said, "Entry for Den",' said Marnie.

Star sighed and grabbed a mop. Making sure the coast was clear, she walked back to the sign at the arched entrance and rubbed away the grime and the dust with the mop to reveal three extra letters: B, I and D.

ENTRY FORBIDDEN

Marnie gulped.

'Well, problem solved,' said Floyd, rubbing his hands together. 'It's forbidden, so we CAN'T go back to the creepy Moon Studies room anyway.'

Marnie sighed. 'Forbidden?' she muttered to herself. 'It's as if everything to do with the moon is forbidden! But why?' Her wings twitched. 'Something VERY weird is going on, and I'm determined to find out what it is!'

CHAPTER 8

SHE GOT CHOMPED

The sun was setting as Marnie headed to her first lesson of the Dark Hours: Predator Studies with none other than Mr Atlas in the Lower Roots of the school. The class sat in complete silence while the teacher handed out their homework sheets. Marnie was horrified – homework before they'd even started the lesson!

'Tonight, we will be learning the top ways to defend ourselves against nocturnal predators. But before we get started, do you have any questions?' he said without any ounce of enthusiasm.

Marnie put her hand up, but the teacher nodded at the small worm with glasses.

'Are we gonna learn about the Early Bird?' asked Gilbert Gubble.

'Yes,' Mr Atlas replied flatly.

'Has the Early Bird ever eaten a teacher?'
Gilbert continued.

Mr Atlas stared at the little worm. 'Not that we
know of,' he said.

'I heard it only eats bad bugs!' Meggitt the
stick insect called out from the ceiling.

'My mother always said that if you're naughty,
the Early Bird will gobble you up!' Veronica
stated with a flap of her bright wings. 'But I never
have to worry, because I'm as good as gold!'

'The Early Bird will attack any bug, good or
bad,' said Mr Atlas grumpily. 'Now, let's get
started . . .'

Marnie put her hand up even higher and waved
it around.

Mr Atlas sighed. 'Yes?'

'Sir, was there a Moon Club at this school?'
asked Marnie.

Mr Atlas flinched. He did NOT look happy to
be asked this particular question.

'The moon has got nothing to do with our lesson,' he replied. 'And it is of no importance to us.'

Marnie gasped, shocked by that response. How could he think that the moon wasn't important? She took a deep breath and raised her hand again, even though her little heart was beating fast.

'Sir, the moon is still really important to lots of bugs!' she said passionately. 'Moonlight helps to guide us. Which is very handy for escaping predators! But it's not just that . . . It could be MAGICAL!'

'Here we go again,' muttered Veronica, who was currently having her antennae glittered by her fellow Betterflies, Thelma and Louise.

'Lunora Wingheart believed in moon magic,' said Marnie desperately. 'AND there might still be the Book of Moon Spells on the moon, left behind by the ancient moths!

Imagine, if somebody found it, we could bring it down to Earth for all the bugs to enjoy together! How exciting would that be?'

'Do you know what happened to Miss Wingheart?' Mr Atlas snapped.

'SHE GOT CHOMPED!' shouted Gilbert
Gubble happily.

'Well, she disappeared,' said Marnie. 'But we
don't know if she really got eat–'

'SILENCE!' Mr Atlas shouted, making Marnie
and the rest of the class jump. A small woodlouse
called William curled up into a ball and rolled out
of the room.

'I'll have NO more mention of Lunora or the
moon OR this utterly ridiculous magic nonsense in

my classroom . . . otherwise you'll be EXPELLED from Minibeast Academy. Do you understand?'

The class was completely silent, apart from a low, alarmed whine coming from the mosquito triplets.

Marnie sank a little lower into her chair, her cheeks burning furiously as the rest of the class stared at her. Expelled? Just for talking about the moon? Her eyes filled with tears and she tried not to cry.

'I will be setting extra homework for you ALL . . .' Mr Atlas snarled. 'And there'll be no more silly moon chat in this classroom.'

As Marnie sniffed sadly, Floyd leaned over and whispered, 'Don't worry – I bet he's just scared you'll know more about the moon than he does.'

Star handed Marnie a scrap of leaf with the words 'ATLAS DESERVES A POKE IN THE BUM' scribbled across it and Marnie gave her a small, sad smile. At least she had Floyd and Star – and now she knew that beneath Star's tough exterior was a kind and loyal friend!

While Mr Atlas made the class read about nocturnal predators in total silence for the rest of the lesson, Marnie doodled little pictures of the moon phases inside her notebook and dreamed about the kinds of magical spells she might be able to do if moon magic was real.

Marnie jumped when the snapdragon snapped to mark the end of the Predator Studies lesson. She'd been doodling absent-mindedly the whole time! She went to close her notebook quickly so that Mr Atlas didn't spot her moon scribbles, but something caught her eye. She'd drawn a small doodle of Lunora on the moon and the words 'HELP ME' above it. Marnie didn't realise she had done that . . . She must've drifted off into her own little world!

There was no time to think about that, though, as Mr Atlas swept his way across the classroom towards her. She tucked her notebook away and made sure not to make eye contact as the grumpy teacher placed EXTRA homework on Marnie's desk.

Marnie soon felt like she was really settling in at Minibeast Academy, although she avoided interacting with Mr Atlas as much as possible. This was just as well, as he really seemed to dislike her and never EVER said so much as a 'well done' for good work.

Little Languages was one of her favourite classes, where she learned the difference between the buzz of a bee and the buzz of a fly (a bee's buzz sounded much friendlier). Marnie went along to a few after-school Webinars, teaching the youngsters how to properly and responsibly use the World Wide Web caller. Oh, and she loved double Night Pollination on a Thursday, especially when they trained on bigwiggle buttercups or hunters honeysuckle – both smelled incredible!

Marnie, Floyd and Star hung out together at break times and always ate together, when Star wasn't scribbling notes in her tiny notebook. One lunchtime, Marnie peered over to see 'IN THE NAME OF MY FATHER, REVENGE WILL BE MINE' scratched on a page in large, angry letters. Marnie's curiosity got the better of her and she cleared her throat. But Floyd got in before her.

'For a tiny ant, you're big on revenge,' he said curiously.

Star frowned. 'So would you if your father, once a MIGHTY KING, was betrayed by his own subjects, lured into a chewing-gum trap and left to the Stompers . . .'

Marnie and Floyd gulped.

'I'm sorry to hear that, Star,' Marnie said gently.

'And there's me thinking being a princess was all sparkles and glam!' said Floyd, trying to lighten the mood.

'It is,' said Star darkly. 'Now, I must finish eating my revenge sandwich.'

'Well, moving swiftly on,' said Floyd lightly. 'We should probably get to class so that Mr Atlas can set us yet MORE homework.' He rolled his eyes.

Marnie sighed. She'd been so excited to start Minibeast Academy and explore her favourite object in the sky. But the moon hadn't been mentioned even ONCE in ANY of her lessons. It was as if it didn't even exist . . .

On a particularly chilly night, Marnie was snuggled in her bed burrow, struggling to sleep. She tossed and turned, catching sight of her Lunora Wingheart poster, which was stuck on the wall opposite.

'I wish I could have met you,' Marnie whispered to the poster. She closed her eyes, trying to imagine what Lunora might have been like in real life.

She pictured the beautiful moonologist standing before her. The imaginary Lunora reached out. Her mouth moved, but Marnie couldn't hear what she was saying. Imaginary Lunora stepped closer, her yellow eyes wide, with a look of . . . was it hope? Then she spoke again and this time Marnie heard the words 'Help me!' before her eyes flicked open to the sound of Floyd shouting from the bed burrow above.

'BEANS ONLY DANCE IF THEY WANT TO!' This was followed by a bump and a scuffle.

A few seconds later, Floyd's head appeared at Marnie's bed burrow. 'Frivolous fruit bats, I'm so sorry I woke you! I have this disturbing recurring dream about beans . . . and, well, we need not elaborate.'

Marnie shook her head and rubbed her eyes. She had obviously fallen asleep . . . but why had her dream felt so real? Why was Lunora's voice still ringing in her mind? And why were her wings tingling?

'Mind if I join you for a little while?' asked Floyd, making himself comfortable beside her. 'It'll be nice to have some company after being chased by killer beans.'

'Did someone say killer beans?'

Star appeared from her bed burrow below, brandishing a human-sized spoon.

'Where are these killer beans?' she asked urgently, eyes narrowed.

'Oh, no, I was just having a nightmare,' Floyd reassured her. 'The killer

beans are only in here . . .' He tapped the side of his head.

'Want me to get them out?' said Star, holding her spoon up a little higher.

'NO!' said Floyd quickly. 'It's all fine, thanks . . . You can put that thing down.'

Star sat next to her friends. Marnie's bed burrow was rather full now, but very cosy!

'Seems like none of us can sleep tonight,' said Marnie. She checked her Dusk-Til-Dawn Dial. 'It's not even sunrise yet. We probably still have quite a while before the morning snapdragon sounds.'

'Are you thinking what I'm thinking?' said Floyd with a cheeky glint in his eyes.

He and Marnie smiled, then both spoke at once.

'Let's go back to the Moon Studies room!' said Marnie.

'Let's crochet,' said Floyd.

Star lowered her spoon and raised an eyebrow.

'You want to go back to the scary room up

the scary stairs where the scary ghost-bug is hanging out?!' asked Floyd, looking a little pale.

'That sounds like a highly satisfying idea,' said Star, sitting up straighter.

Marnie beckoned her friends closer.

'Something WEIRD is going on here at Minibeast Academy – I can sense it,' she whispered. 'And I'm sure there's something inside that forbidden room that can help us.'

Floyd sighed, before tapping each of his elbows and wiggling his antennae.

'Was that waggle code?' asked Marnie.

'That meant: if it'll make you happy, then who am I to stop you . . . ?' he replied.

Marnie fluttered her left wing and wiggled her belly at a very confused-looking Floyd, before tapping her head. 'I saw a bee do this to another bee earlier on . . . I think it's waggle code for "thank you".'

Floyd raised an eyebrow. 'That's definitely not

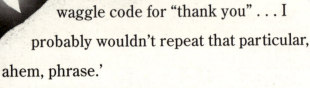

waggle code for "thank you" . . . I probably wouldn't repeat that particular, ahem, phrase.'

'Really?' asked Marnie. 'Wow, this waggle-code stuff is actually super hard!'

Floyd tilted his head to the left and then right, before shimmying three hundred and sixty degrees around the bed burrow.

'What did that mean?'
asked Star.

'It means,' said Floyd with a
grin, 'let's go and explore that
spooky forbidden room!'

❋ CHAPTER 9 ❋
THE TINY FRYING PAN

Minibeast Academy was very quiet. Everyone
was sleeping – even the nocturnal minibeasts.
The whole place felt a lot bigger and scarier with
nobody scurrying around.

Marnie and her friends made their way
through the upper sections of the school until
they reached the dark, forbidden passageway. Up
and around, up and around they went, until they
saw the grimy Moon Studies door. But this time
the door was slightly ajar.

'That door was definitely not open before,'
Floyd whispered. 'Which means someone's been
here!' He paused and added, 'What if they're still
inside?'

'Star, can you use your extra awesome hearing
to check?' asked Marnie.

Star stepped in front and listened carefully.

'No other live individuals present,' she confirmed. 'But I cannot vouch for any non-living creatures in there.'

Floyd's eyes opened so wide that Marnie thought his eyeballs might roll out.

'Come on, it's just a dusty old room,' said Marnie, taking his hand and squeezing it. She took a deep breath. 'Ready?'

As the three friends tiptoed cautiously into the room, they realised that it was positioned in the very top of a mushroom cap at the highest

point of the school. In the ceiling was a large
hole looking out beyond the leaves and into the
night sky.

'WOW!' Marnie breathed. 'I've never seen the
night sky like THIS before!' She almost felt like
crying with happy tears.

Marnie pointed at a small cluster of twinkling
stars above. 'That's the Tiny Frying Pan,' she
said excitedly. 'Also known as the Seven Sisters!
That's my favourite constellation.'

'What's a constellation?' asked Star.

'It's a group of stars that make a pattern, which is usually named after what it looks like. It could be an object, or an animal, or even a mythical figure!' said Marnie. 'Look . . . there's the constellation of Orion with his big, shiny belt in the middle.'

Floyd gasped. 'Is there a constellation of Floyd? With a scarf? I've always thought I'm rather mythical.'

Marnie chuckled. 'If there is, I haven't found it yet!'

She gazed up at the sky once again. The stars were beautiful, but, best of all, there was the big, bright moon: a shaft of silvery light shining down upon the friends. Marnie felt her wings tingle. She was completely drawn to it. How could anyone think it wasn't magical in some way?

'Waxing crescent,' she said wistfully.

'Who's waxing a crescent?' asked Floyd. 'Wait, what's a crescent? Some kind of pastry? And why does it need waxing?'

Marnie burst out laughing. 'No, look!' She pointed up at the moon. 'It's a phase of the moon. When the light part is a crescent shape on the right and the biggest shadowy section is on the left, it's called the waxing crescent phase. It's on its way to becoming a full moon in a couple of weeks.'

Marnie's wings were still tingling. At first, she thought it was the thrill of seeing the moon, but it felt fizzier than that. Marnie couldn't quite explain it.

In the very centre of the room, directly beneath the night-sky viewing point, Star was fiddling with a large and very dusty device.

'This is a very bizarre mechanism,' she mumbled. 'Can I use it in battle?'

'That's a telescope!' gasped Marnie, skipping over, unable to contain her enthusiasm. 'If you look through it, you can get a closer view of things that are really far away, like the moon and stars and planets. I've never seen one this big before!'

She peered through the viewing lens. 'Wow! This is amazing!'

Marnie swept the telescope across the night sky to find the moon, and felt as if she were seeing an old friend. Through the telescope, it looked so much bigger and was covered in lots of shapes and textures. A cluster of stars began dancing like tiny fireflies . . .

Wait . . . dancing? Stars didn't usually dance, did they?

Marnie watched as the stars moved, rearranging themselves. When they stopped, they had created a new constellation . . . But it wasn't a constellation she'd ever seen before. The stars spelled the word 'HELP' . . .

She blinked and suddenly the stars were shining in their original positions again, as if they'd never moved at all.

Marnie stepped back from the telescope. Had her eyes been playing tricks on her?

'That was odd,' she muttered.

'Want to see something really odd?' said Star, pointing to a section of the domed wall. It was covered with several posters and torn-out newspaper articles about the Earthworm Burrowing Trials, which seemed to involve lots of very muscly worms showing off their strength by lifting enormous rocks. Among the papers were also detailed diagrams of pollen-powered jetpacks.

'That is odd,' Floyd agreed.

'Perhaps someone left them behind, back in the

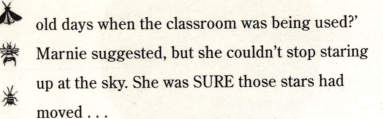

old days when the classroom was being used?'
Marnie suggested, but she couldn't stop staring
up at the sky. She was SURE those stars had
moved . . .

She closed her eyes and took a deep breath
to try to clear her head, but then Marnie saw
the blurry face of Lunora Wingheart: her bright
yellow eyes wide and hopeful. She reached her
arms out to Marnie. 'Please! Stay! I need your
hel–'

'LOOK at this guy!' bellowed Floyd.

Marnie blinked a few times, her wings
tingling fiercely as she was drawn away from
her moondream and back to the reality of the
deserted classroom. Her imagination was in
hyperdrive tonight!

Floyd took down the poster that had got his
attention and handed it to Marnie. It was a
picture of the BIGGEST worm Marnie had ever
seen! Above his picture were the words:

GROUND-BREAKING BURROWING CHAMPION
WITH THE ABILITY TO BURROW
THROUGH EVEN THE TOUGHEST ROCK!

'Fizzling flower beds!' Floyd continued, goggling at yet another poster. 'Marianna Wiggle once burrowed all the way from the North Pole to the South Pole. Now – that's rather impressive.'

'OK, this is just getting weird,' said Marnie. 'Why is an old Moon Studies classroom full of posters of muscly worms and diagrams of pollen-powered jetpacks? And I swear I just saw the stars move!'

'Like shooting stars?' asked Floyd.

'No,' said Marnie. 'Much slower, and they spelled out the word "HELP".'

Star tilted her head to one side. 'Hmm,' she muttered.

'Are you as confused as us?' asked Marnie.

But instead of replying to Marnie's question, Star said calmly, 'I hear footsteps.'

'We shouldn't be here!' squeaked Marnie, looking around for places to hide.

'That's generally what forbidden means,' cried Floyd. 'Oooh, how about hiding here?' he asked, standing behind the World Wide Web caller tucked into the corner.

It looked just like a harp, but with silky strands of spider web instead of strings. At the top was a flowery-shaped speaker for listening and below that, a microphone.

The device did absolutely nothing to hide Floyd – but there was a large bin near it.

'In here!' Marnie hissed, climbing into the bin.

'You've got to be kidding me,' said Floyd.

'Most bugs love bins!' said Star, making herself comfortable.

'As and bees prefer FLOWERS, thank you very much,' retorted Floyd.

But just in the nick of time, Marnie grabbed Floyd's arm and dragged him into the bin.

The footsteps grew louder, then stopped. Whoever – or WHATEVER – it was, they were in the room.

❋ CHAPTER 10 ❋
WHO MISSED THE CAT BUS?

Marnie poked the top of her head out of the bin, being very careful to lower her antennae.

It was hard to see past the weird and wonderful contraptions in the room. There was a rustle and a fumbling around before a deep voice murmured, 'Hmmmm. Where did that go?'

The shadowy figure moved into view. They were wearing a long cloak, with a large hood pulled over their head. Marnie caught a glimpse of the face underneath. She nearly let out a gasp but managed to cover her mouth just in time. She sank lower into the bin and silently mouthed the name to Floyd and Star.

'What?' panic-whispered Floyd. 'Who missed the cat bus?'

Star, who had worked it out, rolled her eyes. Marnie shook her head, then leaned forward and whispered very quietly: 'Mr Atlas!'

Star shoved a hand over Floyd's mouth, covering up his shocked gasp before it had a chance to escape.

What is Mr Atlas doing here? Marnie wondered to herself. *Does he come up here every night? No wonder he is always so tired and grumpy! But why is he here . . . ?*

Walking around the room muttering to himself, the teacher stopped right next to the bin. The friends held their breath, willing him to move

away, but he began plucking at the silky fibres of the World Wide Web caller.

'I do believe the packs are ready . . .' he said into the microphone. There was a pause. 'Yes. There are more than enough earthworms . . .' Mr Atlas laughed lightly, but there was a darkness in his tone. 'Indeed, Alberto. You could say it's the LAST phase of the moon.' He cackled louder this time.

Marnie and the friends looked at each other with wide eyes.

'Yes, almost time now. It's a pleasure, Alberto. I shall see you soon. Goodbye.' There was a zing as the World Wide Web call ended.

Marnie peeped out to see Mr Atlas gliding back across the room. He paused where the Absolute Unit poster had been and frowned.

'Where did it go? Ah well . . .' he muttered, before leaving the room and shutting the door behind him.

Marnie, Floyd and Star stayed very still, until they were sure the coast was clear. With heavy sighs of relief, they clambered out of the bin.

'What was that all about?' asked Floyd.

'I'm as confused as you are,' said Marnie.

Star was busy studying the Burrowing Trials posters in deep thought.

'All these earthworms are known for their extra special abilities to burrow through rock . . .' she said.

'Yeah, they're some of the best burrowing champions of the world,' said Floyd. 'Especially that Absolute Unit dude, whoever he is!'

Marnie retrieved the poster of the Absolute Unit from under her wing and peered at the muscle-bound worm. 'This is all super strange . . .' she said to nobody in particular. 'What did Mr Atlas mean when he said, "You could say it's the last phase of the moon"?'

'Ha ha! Is he gathering some kind of army

of earthworms to burrow into the moon or something?' Floyd said with a chuckle.

There was a silence. The friends looked at each other, and Floyd's smile drooped.

'Bothering beetle-bums . . .' he said slowly, his eyes growing in size.

'HE'S GATHERING AN ARMY OF EARTHWORMS TO BURROW INTO THE MOON!' the friends exclaimed together.

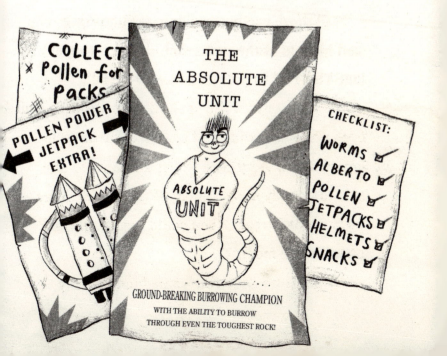

COLLECT Pollen for Packs

POLLEN POWER JETPACK EXTRA!

THE ABSOLUTE UNIT

ABSOLUTE UNIT

GROUND-BREAKING BURROWING CHAMPION
WITH THE ABILITY TO BURROW
THROUGH EVEN THE TOUGHEST ROCK!

CHECKLIST:
WORMS ☑
ALBERTO ☑
POLLEN ☑
JETPACKS ☑
HELMETS ☑
SNACKS ☑

'The packs . . .' said Star. 'He must have meant the jetpacks!'

Marnie felt as if her head was about to explode. This was ridiculous. She looked at the poster in her hands, and her eyes fell upon the last line:

**WITH THE ABILITY TO BURROW
THROUGH EVEN THE TOUGHEST ROCK!**

'If all these earthworms burrow into the moon,' said Marnie as the realisation sank in, 'they'll DESTROY it!'

CHAPTER 11
REALLY, REALLY, REALLY BIG

Before Marnie and her friends had time to think, the morning snapdragon summoned all the students to breakfast. Feeling bleary-eyed and really rather confused, the three friends rushed back to join the other minibeasts, who were beginning to rise from their bed burrows.

Perched on the petals of a daisy, with the chitter-chattering of fellow students around them, it was hard to imagine any of what had just happened had actually . . . happened.

'I can't believe Mr Atlas wants to destroy the moon. He can't do that!' Marnie said in shock.

'Apparently he can,' said Star matter-of-factly.

As Marnie leaned forward to grab some more sap syrup for her porridge, the Absolute Unit poster slipped out from under her wing.

'EEK . . . I forgot that was there!' she squeaked.

'Mr Atlas can't see this, otherwise he'll know we've been sneaking around!'

But before Marnie could hide it, she heard a voice behind her.

'I didn't know you were a fan of my dad!'

It was Gilbert Gubble – and he was pointing at the poster.

'The Absolute Unit is your dad?' asked Marnie in surprise.

'Well, that's not Dad's real name,' Gilbert said, chuckling. 'He's actually called Alberto.

He burrowed right through every rock at Stonehenge, y'know!'

Marnie felt like a firefly had floodlit her brain. 'Alberto . . .' she muttered, then she gasped and immediately tried to contain herself, so as not to give anything away.

'You know what?' she said to Gilbert. 'I AM a fan!'

Gilbert beamed. 'He has his biggest burrowing challenge coming up soon actually,' he said, looking super proud. 'But it's a big secret at the moment. My guess is, he might burrow through something REALLY big, like Mount Everest! Anyway, see you

later,' he said, moving off to get more food.

'Spinning spider webs, Gilbert's dad is Alberto, aka the Absolute Unit!' whispered Marnie, tapping the poster.

'I thought I had family issues . . .' Floyd said, raising an eyebrow. 'But at least my dad isn't about to help Mr Atlas destroy the moon!'

At that moment, Mr Atlas approached the Dining Daisy Chains, his long cloak sweeping out behind him. Marnie hid the poster under her wing and tried to act normal – but she accidentally caught his eye.

Mr Atlas raised an eyebrow, and for the first time ever he smiled just a little bit. 'Good noon to you,' he said as he glided past.

'Is he . . . happy?' said Floyd in disbelief.

'Of course he's happy,' whispered Marnie. 'He hates the moon and now he's about to destroy it. We have to stop him!'

'How?!' asked Floyd.

'Death,' said Star bluntly.

'No, no . . . that's not necessary,' Marnie added quickly. 'But let's keep a close eye on Mr Atlas from now on. We need to keep track of everywhere he goes.'

'Everywhere, as in *everywhere*?' asked Floyd. 'Even the toilet?'

'Eww, no!' said Marnie. 'We just need to make sure he doesn't leave Minibeast Academy, so he can't sneak off and destroy the moon . . .'

☙✷ CHAPTER 12 ✷❧
SAVE THE MOON!

Botany class was the last lesson before lunch
time. It was held in a large conker decorated
with lots of pictures of different types of flowers.
She had never even heard of some, such as the
bearded acquaintance, stepdad's work-week and
the temperamental snozzle-poppy wort-head. But
Marnie couldn't concentrate on the lesson at all.
All she could think about was Mr Atlas!

'What direction do sunflowers face during the
day and the night?' asked Miss Pudge, a very
shiny beetle with the longest, pointiest head
horn Marnie had ever seen!

Veronica's hand shot straight up.

'Marnie Midnight? Would you care to answer
for us?' asked the teacher.

Marnie blinked and dropped her pencil.

'Um . . .' She tried to look as if she had the

answer on the tip of her tongue. The truth was, she hadn't listened to one word of the lesson so far.

'Miss, miss! I know!' said Veronica, waving a hand around impatiently. 'During daytime sunflowers follow the sun westward across the sky, and at night-time they face east again. And when they get old, they stay facing east, waiting for us to spread their pollen.'

'Thank you for that, Veronica,' said the beetle teacher. 'But I was asking Marnie here.' Miss Pudge scurried over to her, smiling sweetly. 'It looked as though you were writing lots of useful notes on today's lesson, Marnie. May I see them?'

'Uh, um . . .' Marnie stammered.

Marnie was beginning to wonder if she was capable of saying anything else. The thing is, she had been writing notes, but they certainly had nothing to do with anything that had been taught in the Botany lesson so far.

Miss Pudge picked up Marnie's notebook. She stared at Marnie's elaborate scribbles of Mr Atlas stuck in a spider web, and a very detailed illustration of Marnie, Floyd and Star shouting, 'WE'LL SAVE THE MOON!'

The teacher turned back through the pages to find more sketches of the various ways in which the friends could prevent Mr Atlas from destroying the moon. While Star's suggestions often resulted in a very gruesome end, Floyd was determined to weave the element of song into their plan.

'THIS,' said Miss Pudge, sounding less jolly than she had, 'is an example of what NOT to do in class.' She frowned at Marnie, then at Floyd and Star. 'The three of you will stay in over lunchtime as punishment.'

Sunflowers follow the sun from east to west and I will listen from now on.

Marnie felt her eyes drooping as she wrote the sentence for the fiftieth time . . . but she still had to write it another four hundred times. Detention was so boring, and the detention lunch was even worse! But that wasn't all. Her next Predator Studies lesson would be starting soon. How could she face Mr Atlas and act as if everything was fine and dandy?

Sunflowers follow the sun from east to west and I will listen from now on.

Sunflowers follow the sun from east to west and I will listen from now on.

Sunflowers follow the sun from east to west and I will listen from now on.

Sunflowers follow the sun from east to west and I will listen from now on.

Sunflowers follow the sun from east to l

Faster and faster, Marnie kept writing her lines
. . . although her wings were tingling SO much it
was distracting her!

Sunflowers follow the sun from east
to west and I will listen from now on.

Sunflowers follow the sun from east
to west and I will listen from now on.

Sunflowers HELP the sun from east
to west and I AM from now on.

Sunflowers HELP the sun from east
to west and I AM ON.

Wait a minute, thought Marnie as she stared
down at the page. She hadn't written that . . . had
she? She wrote another line.

HELP the sun from east to west and I AM
ON THE sunflowers.

Then another . . .

HELP ME THE MOON I AM ON
THE sunflowers.

And another . . .

HELP ME I AM ON THE MOON.

Marnie gasped and dropped her pencil.
She was writing her lines, but the words were
definitely NOT the words she thought she was
writing down. It was as though her hands had a
life of their own!

'Everything OK over there, Miss Midnight?'
asked Miss Pudge.

Marnie straightened herself up and nodded as if nothing weird was going on, before picking up her pencil again. Her hand was trembling as she paused above the page to write another line, her wings tingling furiously.

Floyd leaned over from his desk. 'Marnie, are you all right?' he whispered.

'I . . . I think . . . the words . . . I think . . .' Marnie stammered. Her mind was swirling. She carried on writing, feeling as if she were hypnotised.

HELP ME, I AM ON THE MOON.

There was a loud SNAP, SNAP, SNAP as the snapdragon signalled the end of lunch.

Marnie shook her head and stared at the page of absolute nonsense in front of her.

'What on earthworm?!' she squeaked.

'I hope you've all had a chance to think about your actions,' said Miss Pudge. 'Now get off to your next lesson. And let's have no more of this silliness.'

The friends left the classroom in silence. Marnie made sure they were far enough away before blurting out: 'HELP ME, I AM ON THE MOON!'

Floyd and Star stared at their friend, eyes wide.

'Um . . . I don't think you are,' said Floyd, putting an arm around her wing and sounding concerned.

'I wrote this!' Marnie squeaked, showing them her notebook. 'But I DIDN'T write it!'

Star for once looked confused and slightly worried. 'Should we call the nit nurse?'

'No! Listen,' said Marnie urgently. 'When we were writing our lines, something really strange happened. My wings started to tingle and I ended up writing THIS. I think . . . I think something happened to me,' she continued, trying to make sense of it all. 'It's almost as if someone else had control of me!'

'Well, that doesn't sound normal,' said Floyd. 'Are you sure you weren't just moondreaming? I wouldn't blame you. That detention was very boring!'

'No, I was definitely awake,' said Marnie. 'It's hard to describe, but it felt . . . *magical*. Then the snapdragon snapped and it all went away.'

Star took the notebook. Her antennae twitched curiously. 'What could it mean?'

'I . . . I think . . .' Marnie started, hardly able to believe the words that were about to leave her mouth. 'I'm not sure how, but I think someone has been trying to talk to me. I think this might be the work of moon magic!'

❀ CHAPTER 13 ❀
THIS IS NOT A DRILL!

'Moon magic?' Floyd repeated. 'Like, actual MAGIC?'

Marnie bit her lip, her wings tingling again, this time from excitement. 'I . . . I don't know for sure. But I think so. I felt hypnotised and my wings were tingling so much!'

'Oh, mine are tingling too!' said Floyd, then he paused. 'But that usually just means I have trapped wind.'

'We didn't need to know that,' Star said with a sigh.

Marnie felt her little heart begin to beat faster. 'I've been having these strange moondreams too . . . day and night.'

'Like visions?' asked Star.

'Maybe . . .' replied Marnie. 'Sometimes my

mind wanders and Lunora will be there,
reaching out and asking for help . . . It always
feels SO real.'

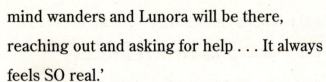

Star grinned. 'Cool!'

'And through the telescope I saw the stars
spell out "HELP",' Marnie continued. 'I thought
my eyes were playing tricks on me, but maybe,
just maybe, I'm not imagining these things?'

'What are you saying?' said Floyd.

'If these messages are real, then what if it is
Lunora and she's alive?! What if she's somehow
using MOON MAGIC to communicate?' Marnie's
heart skipped a beat.

'I thought Lunora disappeared years ago,'
said Floyd.

'Gobbled by the Early Bird, so the rumours
go,' added Star.

'Yes, everybody thinks that, but nobody knows
for sure,' said Marnie, shaking her head. 'This
is real, though. I can FEEL it. What if Lunora

did make it to the moon after all? But, for some reason, couldn't get back home?'

The friends looked at each other for a moment before the realisation sank in.

'Um . . . I don't suppose it would be the same moon Mr Atlas wants to . . . y'know . . . destroy?' asked Floyd awkwardly.

Marnie's blood ran cold, as though her heart had frozen over. 'We have to talk to him right now and get him to STOP!'

The three friends flutter-ran to Predator Studies in the Lower Roots of the school. But to Marnie's surprise, Mr Atlas wasn't there. In his place was a jittery old centipede called Miss Scrigglesworth, formerly the leader of the local Pest Party for the Botanical Gardens Council, according to Floyd.

'Um, miss, where's Mr Atlas?' Marnie asked urgently.

'He's come down with inflamed philtrum,'

croaked Miss Scrigglesworth. 'Now, take your seats – you are all late!'

'That can't possibly be right,' said Marnie. 'Moths don't HAVE a philtrum!'

Just then an ear-piercingly loud voice echoed through the walls of the school.

'ALERT! ALERT! ALERT!

EARLY BIRD! EARLY BIRD! EARLY BIRD!'

'It might just be a drill,' said Floyd hopefully.

'THIS IS NOT A DRILL!!

ALERT! ALERT! ALERT!'

The class erupted into chaos – clearly not remembering anything from their Early Bird drills in which they were taught to STAY CALM!

'Class! Calm down! You must form an orderly line so I can take you down to the Bug Bunker!' bellowed the teacher.

'This is scary!' cried Floyd.

'This is thrilling!' said Star, laughing manically.

'This is suspicious,' said Marnie, narrowing her eyes. 'It's night-time, not morning . . . This is Mr Atlas's work, I bet!' she exclaimed, before grabbing Floyd and Star's hands and dragging them away from the commotion.

'Marnie, we have to go the bunker!' shrieked Floyd, his voice MUCH higher than usual.

'We don't need to go to the bunker,' said Marnie. 'I don't think this is a real alert!'

Star nodded. 'It makes sense. With the whole school being sent to the Bug Bunker, it's the perfect opportunity for Mr Atlas to carry out his plan without anyone noticing.'

'Yes!' agreed Marnie. 'If the earthworms

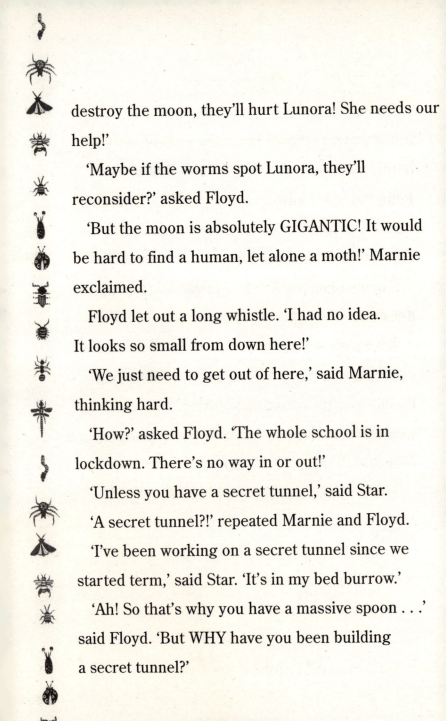

destroy the moon, they'll hurt Lunora! She needs our help!'

'Maybe if the worms spot Lunora, they'll reconsider?' asked Floyd.

'But the moon is absolutely GIGANTIC! It would be hard to find a human, let alone a moth!' Marnie exclaimed.

Floyd let out a long whistle. 'I had no idea. It looks so small from down here!'

'We just need to get out of here,' said Marnie, thinking hard.

'How?' asked Floyd. 'The whole school is in lockdown. There's no way in or out!'

'Unless you have a secret tunnel,' said Star.

'A secret tunnel?!' repeated Marnie and Floyd.

'I've been working on a secret tunnel since we started term,' said Star. 'It's in my bed burrow.'

'Ah! So that's why you have a massive spoon . . .' said Floyd. 'But WHY have you been building a secret tunnel?'

'You never know when you might need a secret tunnel,' Star replied nonchalantly. 'But only part of the way is secret. My tunnel connects to the Pong Passage – the dung delivery route – which travels out of the school, under the pond and into the garden of the museum.'

Floyd looked horrified. 'Did you say DUNG delivery?'

'Affirmative,' said Star.

'We need to find Mr Atlas fast, so we can save Lunora and the moon!' said Marnie, flapping her wings with determination and almost knocking over Star. 'TO THE SECRET TUNNEL!'

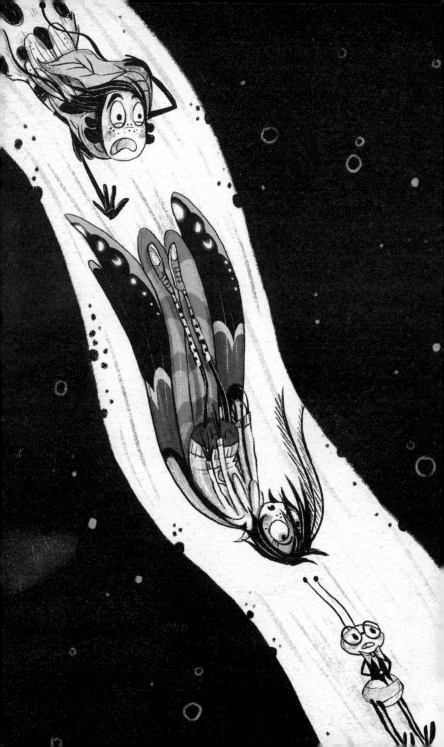

CHAPTER 14

BEEN THERE, DUNG THAT

Marnie was crawling through the teensy (ant-sized) tunnel for what seemed like a very long time, when the tunnel suddenly took a steep dive and the smell of dung became overpowering. Marnie found herself sliding downwards at full speed.

'We're now sliding along the Pong Passage!' Star yelled from the front.

'YOU DON'T SAY!' Floyd replied. 'Wait . . . what if there's a delivery on its way while we're in here?'

Thankfully there wasn't.

Moments later, the three friends emerged with a POP, POP, SPLAT!

Star and Marnie managed to avoid landing in the pile of dung balls awaiting delivery. Floyd did not.

He stood up slowly and brushed himself down.

'This is all very unpleasant,' he said, swaying, his usually immaculate wings crumpled and stained. 'Never thought I'd be rolling around in the Pong Passage to save the moon when I started at Minibeast Academy.'

'You could say you've been there, DUNG that!' Marnie said, grinning.

Floyd couldn't help laughing. 'My life has definitely been far more interesting since meeting you, Marnie Midnight!'

The three little bugs made their way out into

the cold night air.

Marnie gazed up at the sky, admiring the sparkling stars and the bright crescent moon.

'Don't worry, Lunora,' she said with determination. 'I'm not going to let anything happen to you.'

'We should probably make sure nothing happens to us too,' Floyd squeaked. 'We're exposed to the elements here . . . AND hungry predators!'

The friends looked around them. They were not on school grounds any more. It was both

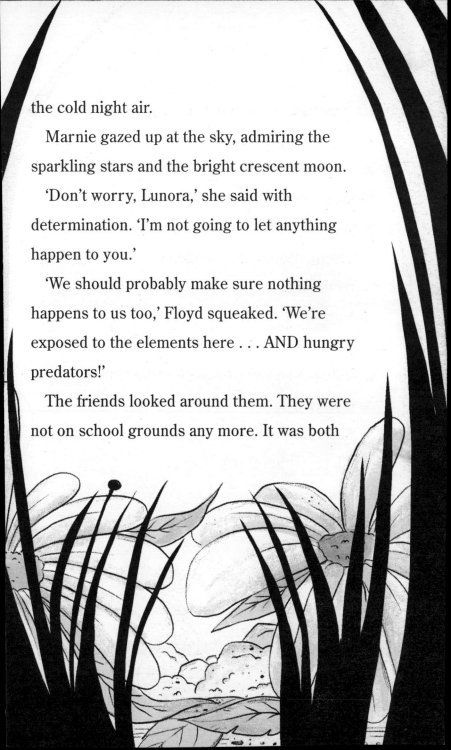

exciting and terrifying!

'How do we know which way to go?' asked Floyd. 'And where are we going?'

Marnie had to admit she had no idea.

'We need to find Mr Atlas . . .' She scratched her head. 'Come on, Marnie,' she muttered to herself. 'THINK'.

A few grass blades away, a worm with a briefcase slid past, looking as though he was in a rush, but stealing a glance at the three friends in concern.

'Minibeast Academy is THAT way,' he said, nodding behind them.

Marnie gulped.

'We're on a research trip!' Star called out to reassure the worm.

Then, all of a sudden, she whipped out the Absolute Unit poster that had been stashed beneath Marnie's wing.

'Can you tell us where to find the Absolute

Unit?' the little ant asked politely with a sweet smile. 'It's for our very important research.'

The businessworm looked a little less concerned and a bit more confused. 'The education system has sure changed since I was at school,' he muttered, then more clearly he said, 'The Absolute Unit has a training base in Miniopolis; you'll probably find him there.'

'Thank you so much, kind sir!' said Star, sounding completely UNLIKE the Star that Marnie knew. She gave the worm a firm salute and headed into the tall grasses away from the school.

Floyd and Marnie looked at each other with wide eyes, before running to catch up with Star.

'We should probably have asked that worm which way the city is!' said Marnie.

'No need. The city of Miniopolis is south of the Minibeast Academy,' Star declared. 'I remember seeing it on the maps in the Ant Military Base. So if we can work out which way is south . . .'

'The moon!' Marnie gasped, looking up at her favourite object in the sky. 'We can use the moon to guide us!'

'But we know nothing about Moon Navigation,' said Floyd.

'I do!' said Marnie proudly.

She looked up at the moon and put her skills to the test. She thought carefully.

'OK, this won't be PERFECTLY accurate, but it will give us a good idea which direction is south.' She pointed up towards the crescent moon. 'Imagine a line connecting the two points of the moon . . . then keep that line going all the way to the horizon . . .' She moved her arm along this imaginary line. 'Where the line meets the horizon should be south!'

'Now that IS impressive,' said Floyd.

The friends walked in a southerly direction through the grasses, passing gigantic sunflowers illuminated by the lights pouring through the large windows of the Museum of Nature.

'Look!' said Floyd, pointing upwards.

SOUTH!

'Remember what we were told in Botany class? The sunflowers will be facing east overnight, waiting for the sunrise, so we can use them to help guide us too.'

'Great thinking, Floyd!' cheered Marnie, feeling grateful for nature helping them to find their way.

They passed the huge, bright green leaves of a pondering periwinkle and the tall, triangular leaves of Floyd's favourite flower, the great crested bedstead. But soon their surroundings became less green – and a lot spikier and scary looking.

The friends approached a ragged twig archway, with a sign that read: NETTLE LANES.

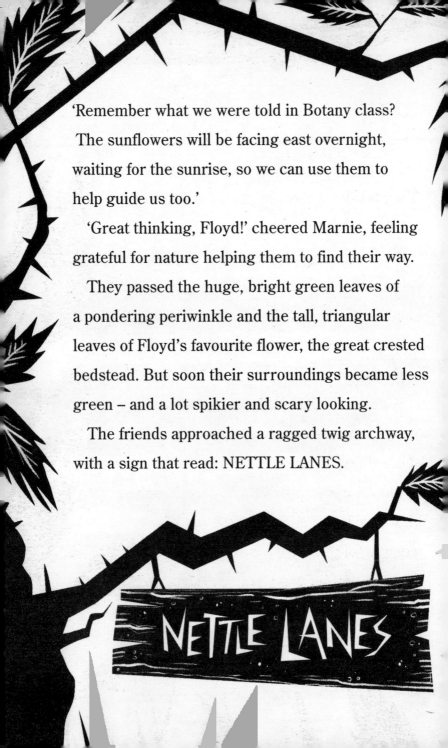

NETTLE LANES

'This doesn't look like the kind of place we should be passing through,' said Floyd.

'I've heard about the Nettle Lanes,' said Star. 'They border the side of the museum near where the Stampers' bins are kept.'

Peering through the archway, the grass very quickly turned into a twisting network of prickly passages, lined with tooth-edged leaves.

Marnie bit her lip.

'We can't go that way,' Floyd whispered. 'It looks like the kind of place the creepiest of crawlies hang out.'

'But if we don't carry on, then we won't be able to save Lunora and the moon in time!' said Marnie. 'Is there another way?' she asked Star.

'I don't know,' said Star.

The friends were quiet for a moment.

'Being good at flying would really help right now. I can only manage a low flutter,' said Marnie.

She flapped her wings, feeling her feet lift off of the ground. She tried to remember what she'd been learning in Flying Practice . . . *Try not to think about it too much otherwise you'll get too caught up in THINKING rather than FLYING and fall to the ground.*

BOSH.

That is exactly what happened.

Marnie sighed, then took a deep breath. 'We're just going to have to be brave,' she said.

Floyd shuffled on the spot uncomfortably, but Star saluted and cried out, 'Let's do this!'

'I want to, but I'm really scared,' whispered Floyd.

Marnie took Floyd's trembling hand.

'We're in this together,' she said kindly. 'I won't leave your side. Promise.'

Floyd managed a small smile before twitching his right antenna, clicking his fingers three times, tapping his left foot twice and wiggling his bottom.

'That means "thank you",' he said with a smile.

Before they knew it, the friends were scurrying as fast as their multiple legs could carry them through the Nettle Lanes.

There was a deep buzzing sound nearby. And it wasn't the friendly hum of a bumblebee kind of buzz.

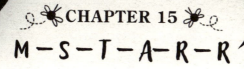

CHAPTER 15

M – S – T – A – R – R

Marnie widened her eyes and stopped mid-run.

'Flies,' she said fearfully.

'Flies?!' squeaked Floyd. 'Now is the time I wish I were part spider!'

Trying not to draw attention to themselves, the friends tiptoed past a rather rowdy pub called the Hornet's Hub and an illegal sting-replacement store.

Marnie spotted two shifty-looking flies watching the friends closely.

'All right, you three?' said one of the flies.

Marnie's little heart began to beat faster.

'Keep walking,' she whispered. Floyd squeezed her hand tighter.

But Marnie soon found the two flies blocking their way. One was tall and spindly, while the other was short and round; both were wearing peak caps and blazers.

'Bad manners ter ignore yer elders,' said the stout fly. 'Don't ya fink so, Mildew?'

'Yeah, we were just trying ter be nice, weren't we, Mould?' said the spindly fly called Mildew.

'We have places we need to be,' said Star stiffly. She attempted to walk past, but the pair of flies took a step to the side, still blocking her way.

'Not often ya see a tiny little ant like yerself with a clumsy moth and badly dressed bee 'round these parts,' Mould jeered.

Floyd tutted. 'Firstly, I'm not a bee, I'm an A, and well . . .' He poked his left bottom cheek, then his right.

'What did you just call me?' bellowed Mould, lurching forward. 'Yeah, that's right, I learned a bit o' waggle code in me maggot days! We are fine, eradicated fellows, don't ya know?'

'You mean educated!' whispered Mildew.

Mould narrowed his eyes at Floyd before

flicking his long proboscis and stamping his
left foot once.

'You did NOT just say that!' Floyd gasped, and
reached for his pearls to clutch, but they weren't
there! 'Where are my pearls? You've taken them!'

'I dunno what yer talking about,' said Mildew,
placing the pearls around his neck.

'Hey! Give my friend's necklace back!' said Marnie, trying to act as stern as possible, even though her legs were shaking like a leaf.

'Finders keepers,' said Mildew. 'Could get a few scraps of meat for this – what d'ya reckon, Mould?'

Mould rubbed his hands together hungrily. 'We can get more than a few scraps!' He studied the glimmering pearls. 'We could get RICH!'

'Congratulations, guys,' said Star. 'Now let us pass.'

'I can't leave without my pearls!' Floyd hissed. 'They're my special pearls for clutching when I'm shocked!'

The two flies cackled loudly.

Marnie suddenly had an idea.

'I think you'll find you're disrespecting a princess of the Seven Ant Hills . . .' She folded her arms. 'That's treason! Therefore you must let us pass.'

But the flies cackled EVEN LOUDER, now doubled over laughing.

'You fink us flies are bothered 'bout a bunch o' royal ants?' said Mildew.

Marnie frowned, deflated.

To her surprise, though, Star was smiling. 'Oh well, I guess I won't offer you a healthy sum of golden grains then . . .'

Mould and Mildew stopped laughing. They both raised their eyebrows, looking interested.

'Why, er, what d'ya mean . . . offer us?' said Mould, adjusting his blazer and attempting to make himself look taller.

'How many golden grains are we talking 'ere?' asked Mildew, a sparkle in his eye.

'You seem like the kind who might like a good deal,' Star continued, now she had their full attention – though Marnie had NO idea what her plan was, and really hoped this *was* part of a plan.

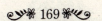

'Depends on the deal, princess,' said Mould with a sly grin.

Star cleared her throat. 'If you spell my name correctly, I'll give you twenty thousand golden grains. You have three chances.'

'An' if we don't spell it right?' asked Mildew.

Star shrugged. 'You let us pass. Simple. Oh, and you lead us safely to the Burrowing Champion's training base in Miniopolis. And, you return my friend's pearls.'

The two flies guffawed and snorted. 'All right . . . What's ya name, kid?'

'My name is Star.'

The flies looked at each other and grinned. 'Well, this is gonna be easy!'

'What are you doing?'

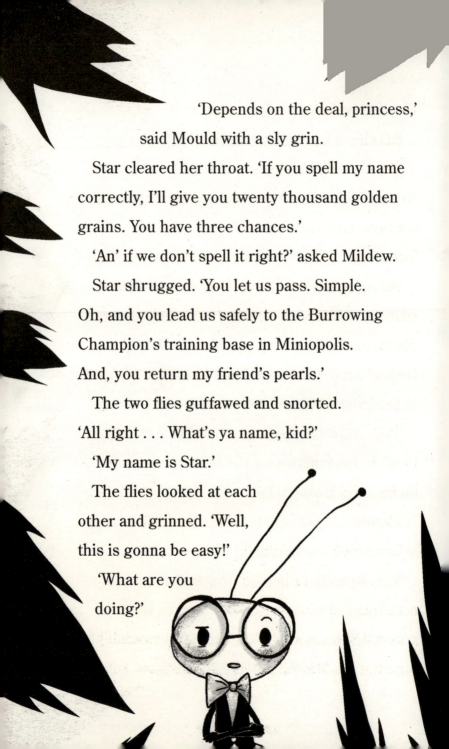

Floyd hissed in Star's direction.

'Making a fair deal,' she replied.

Marnie didn't know how Star seemed so confident right now! It took all of Marnie's courage not to run off in the opposite direction . . .

'All right then, Princess Star,' said Mildew, spatters of spit narrowly missing Marnie's face. 'Ya name is spelled like this. S – T – A – R.' He was about to cheer with glee.

'Incorrect,' Star replied. The fly slumped.

'Nah, Mildew, it's clearly got two Rs, ya big turd! All royalty 'ave two Rs!' said Mould, hands on hips. He looked at Star. 'It's S – T – A – R – R . . . innit?'

'Incorrect,' said Star.

Marnie thought hard and then she remembered what she had spotted on the cover of Star's notebook in their first assembly together . . . Marnie felt like shouting out with joy but kept quiet.

Mould and Mildew looked at each other in confusion.

'Mate!' Mildew shrieked. 'There's CLEARLY a silent M in it . . . All the best names have a silent M. Like mine.'

'Your name is Mildew – that's not a silent M,' Mould replied flatly.

But Mildew ignored his partner in crime and proudly said, 'Star is spelled M – S – T – A – R – R.'

Mould put his head in his hands.

'That was your last chance,' said Star, plucking her birth certificate from seemingly nowhere. There it was. A five-pointed little star representing her name.

'You have GOT to be kidding me,' said Mould with a groan.

'A deal's a deal, lads,' said Star, tucking her certificate away. 'Who's leading the way?'

CERTIFICATE OF BIRTH

★

NAME: _____

DATE: _Midwinter Monday_

PLACE: _Anthill Infirmary_

VII

CHAPTER 16
TRASHFORD

Marnie gazed up at the huge cylindrical towers rising above them as Mould and Mildew led the way onwards, grumbling to themselves. The buzzing coming from inside the towers was extremely loud, and pieces of rotten food lay scattered on the ground, surrounded by scraggly flies and wasps and nasty-looking bugs.

'Welcome to Trashford!' said Mould proudly. 'Three of the biggest and BEST bins around. And also the best ride you'll ever get.' He waltzed over to a small door at the bottom of the bin at the end and shouted, 'AUUUUDREEEEY.'

The little door creaked open, and then, to Marnie, Floyd and Star's utter horror, a huge rat squidged through the gap.

Floyd seized his scarf and screamed, 'I NEED TO CLUTCH MY PEARLS!'

Marnie felt as if her feet had been stuck to the ground with the stickiest sap – she was well and truly frozen to the spot.

Star growled (Marnie didn't think ants could do that!) and narrowed her eyes at Mould and Mildew.

'We had a DEAL,' she said sternly. 'And now you're feeding us to the RATS?!'

The rat looked offended. 'Now hold on a strawberry-picking minute – I'm vegan!'

Mould and Mildew patted their friend soothingly. 'We're sorry, Audrey. Our new acquaintances 'ere aren't used to being so close to your kind.'

Mould then turned to the young minibeasts. 'Audrey means ya no harm,' he said

reassuringly. 'She's the most
reliable taxi service in
Trashford. Can
get ya across ter
t'other side of the
museum in less than five minutes!'

Marnie gawped. That was HUNDREDS of
minibeast miles and would be impossible for
a bug on their own, especially ones that couldn't
fly too well yet!

'We met Audrey when she was just a teeny
rat,' said Mould. 'Grown up with us in the Third
Bin, ent ya? Like a daughter to us. Was a right
nightmare in 'er teen years but grew up into a
radiant beauty, eh!'

Marnie stared at the three-legged, scraggly
rodent with half of an ear chewed off.

'Now she's all grown up an' successful with 'er
own Ratsy Taxi business! Bloomin' perfect for
me an' Mould,' said Mildew. 'An' lots of the other

trade-flies 'round 'ere.'

'What could possibly require so many Ratsy Taxi journeys?' asked Floyd.

'Oh, y'know . . . trading goods,' said Mildew.

'What kinds of goods?' asked Marnie, grimacing at the smell of the bins.

'Just illegal goods,' said Mould casually. 'Right, hop on to Audrey's back, or else you won't get to ya destination any time soon – an' it sounds like yer in a hurry!'

Never in a buzzillion years did Marnie imagine she'd be riding on the back of a rat with two dodgy flies who actually turned out to be quite nice . . . Yet here she was!

Audrey scurried through a winding alley covered in spider webs, over an attraction named 'Biggest Compost Heap in the WORLD,' under at least three Stomper benches, and past a famous minibeast restaurant called The Hungry Caterpillar (owned by Mould and Mildew's other brother Eric). The rat stopped just outside a huge bush covered in large

purple berries that surrounded the gardens
of the Museum of Nature.

'OK, kids. Beyond the baffleberry bushes
you'll find Miniopolis. You can't miss it. But this is
as far as we can go,' said Mould finally.

'Isn't there a way into the city that doesn't
require passing through the bushes where the
Early Bird loves to hang out?' squeaked Floyd.

''Fraid we can't use the proper entrance,'
said Mould.

'There may be a small chance we're wanted
in certain parts of Miniopolis,' Mildew added.
'But if yer swift, ya prob'ly won't get eaten.
The Burrowing Champion's training base is on
Pickapetal Lane.'

'Thank you for getting us this far,' said Marnie,
jumping off Audrey's back.

'I'm not saying thank you until I emerge from that
bush in one piece,' grumbled Floyd.

'Hope ter see youse kids again,' said Mould.

'An' 'ere . . .' called Mildew, tossing Floyd's pearl necklace through the air towards him. 'I fink you're prob'ly gonna need it.'

Floyd hugged the pearls to his chest gratefully, as the flies saluted the three friends before buzzing off.

'Well, that was all very weird,' said Floyd.

Marnie kept her breathing steady as the friends walked among the huge spikes and tangled prickles of the baffleberry bush. The jumble of leaves, thorns and sleeping blooms towered above the little bugs, blocking out any ounce of light from the moon.

Star used her super-duper hearing to make sure there were no unexpected predators creeping up on them.

'I hear the faint hum of bustling bugs,' she whispered.

'Phew!' said Marnie, letting her wings relax a little. 'That means we're almost at Miniopolis!'

A sliver of moonlight shone through as the bush began to thin out, almost as if reassuring Marnie everything was going to be OK. As long as the moon was there, Marnie felt safe. Even better, she felt brave!

Before long, the thick, woody stems of the baffleberry bush thinned out enough to reveal a whole bug kingdom. It was BUSY and literally buzzing with

minibeasts of
all kinds on the
move. A network of vines,
shoots and stalks connected
hundreds of colourful flower huts,

surrounding a huge water fountain that stretched up high above everything else.

Marnie could hardly take it in. There was everything here – hotels, restaurants and shops, all joined up by the Beetle Bus line. Marnie watched as day and night bugs rode by on a tour-slug, heading to the West End district, while a group of wasps were protesting for equal flights to bees.

There was a CRUNCH from behind them.

'What was that?' Floyd whispered.

'I don't know,' Marnie answered, looking around for signs of other bugs within the bush. A flicker of nervous energy prickled her wings. 'But we should keep moving . . .'

CRUNCH.

Marnie grimaced. She held Floyd's hand a little tighter and tried her best to keep a brave face on for her friends . . . Well, mostly for Floyd. Star didn't seem to be scared of anything!

CRUNCH!

'I don't think a bug makes a crunch THAT loud!' squeaked Floyd.

The friends ran towards Miniopolis, but the small sliver of moonlight leading their way through the stems and thorns was suddenly replaced by a dark shadow.

'Um, Marnie . . .' Floyd barely whispered.

'Don't worry, it's probably just a cloud,' said Marnie.

But then she heard the flapping of wings. The dark silhouette of something large with a pointy beak loomed towards them. There was only one thing it could be.

The Early Bird.

CHAPTER 17

SHARON

Marnie blinked her eyes open slowly. Everything was dark. Was she . . . inside the stomach of the Early Bird?

But Marnie was surprised to find that all her limbs were still attached to her body, and it didn't feel very stomach-y either. She'd imagined the inside of a bird's belly would be much squishier and wetter, but beneath her was a hard surface.

'Marnie? Are you there?' called Floyd's voice.

'FLOYD!' she gasped, reaching out for her friend. She squeezed his shoulder tight.

'This is Star, and that's my head you're squeezing,' said the voice of the little ant.

'My eyes haven't adjusted, so I can't see you!' said Marnie. 'Are you both OK?'

'I don't know,' said Floyd. 'ARE WE?'

A BOMP made the friends jump, before a

small candle flame was lit nearby, illuminating what appeared to be the inside of an old attic. The place was decorated with all sorts of strange items Marnie had only ever read about in books about the Swatters. She did, however, recognize one of the items – a large teacup with the words 'WORLD'S BEST BOSS' written on it. From behind the teacup emerged the back of a gigantic brown-feathered bird.

'Teatime . . . !' the bird sang.

'PLEASE DON'T EAT US!' cried Marnie, spreading her wings out in front of Floyd and Star to protect them. 'We're terribly bland and probably very bad for your health!'

'Hey, I'm nourishing!' said Floyd. There was a BOSH and a jingle as Star poked him in the antenna to shush him.

The bird turned round, revealing a large white belly with a bright orange chest. And it appeared to be holding . . . a plate of crisp crumbs?

'Oh . . . are crumbs not nourishing?' said the bird, suddenly looking concerned. 'I'm so sorry, the last bug I collected claimed they loved a good crisp crumb! We always find tons on the museum floors.'

Floyd's antennae flickered. 'Depends what flavour crumb,' he said, which was met by another bosh from Star.

'Oh, these crumbs are a flavour I can't even pronounce,' the bird replied, offering the plate to the friends. 'Something like woos . . . No, wait, woosta . . . Hmmm, wooster-ser . . . shur . . . sauce flavour, I think. Anyhoo, what are you three running from?'

'Um . . . you?' Floyd answered.

The bird chortled. 'ME? Why me?'

'Because you want to eat us for BREAKFAST,' Floyd shrieked.

'Whatever gave you that idea?' asked the bird, looking surprised. 'I don't eat bugs. And anyway, I'm allergic to dairy, so I couldn't eat you even if I wanted to.'

Marnie felt like her brain was turning inside out. All she could respond with was: 'I didn't know I contained dairy.'

'How rude of me! I've not properly introduced myself!' said the bird, ruffling her feathers. 'I'm Sharon, the Robin of the Night!'

Marnie finally found her voice. 'YOU'RE the Early Bird!' she gawped.

Sharon tilted her head to one side. 'Oh, is that what they call me now? I always assumed I was known as the Christmas Bird,' she said wistfully. 'Not sure why, though. I'm here all year! But I do love Christmas . . . Do you like Christmas?'

Marnie blinked a few times. Was this really happening?

'So you're NOT going to eat us?' Floyd double-checked, looking a bit sickly. 'Or is this just a big trick to lure us in, then MUNCH us up!'

Sharon chuckled. 'You, sir, sound like you've been listening to too many *True Grime* stories! In fact, I am the ultimate travel service for bugs that wish to go on adventures far away – I'm part of a group called the Escape-bees. Bugs desiring to travel must wait within the baffleberry bushes bordering the kingdom on the first Friday of every month. But, of course, you must know this already, if you were waiting for me . . . weren't you?' she asked.

'Um, no,' said Marnie, her limbs still feeling a little numb from the shock of facing what she had thought was her demise.

'I've heard of the Escape-bees,' said Star thoughtfully. 'They're a criminal organisation for those who want to run from the law . . . to "disappear", then change their identity. I think you'll find you've been helping law-breaking minibeasts!'

'How do you know that?' asked Floyd.

Star raised an eyebrow. 'Classified.'

Sharon looked shocked. 'Don't be silly. I've been helping innocent bugs go on big adventures, just like my parents used to. They did it for years!'

'Is this your collection of travellers?' asked Marnie, pointing to the many photos of shady-looking bugs that covered the walls.

'Yes,' said Sharon, her eyes wide with confusion. 'They brought me treats like golden grains.' She gestured to the pile of sparkling gold in the corner of the attic.

Star pointed to the first picture. 'I think you'll find that is Jittery Jimbo, the centipede who stole one hundred sacks of golden grains from the Mines of Miniopolis.'

'Oh! I've definitely seen him in my dad's *Daily Buggle* newspaper . . .' Marnie added.

Star moved on to the next picture. 'That there is Sneaky Susan, the spider who used to trap butterflies and steal their wings . . .'

Sharon gasped.

'And that's Vera,' said Star, tapping another picture. 'You don't want to even know what Vera got up to.'

Sharon was looking positively stunned. She sat down slowly. Marnie had never seen a bird 'sit' before. In fact, there was a quite a lot she hadn't experienced before this particular trip.

'Wiggling wingspans,' said Sharon quietly. 'I always thought I was being helpful.'

'You've definitely been helpful . . . to criminals,' said Floyd rather unhelpfully.

Marnie suddenly had a brilliant idea.

'You know, you can still help others. Lots and lots of good bugs could do with the help of a helpful robin like you!' she said with a smile. 'In fact, my friends and I could really do with your help right now.'

Sharon's eyes became brighter. 'It would be
wonderful to help out good bugs rather than
naughty ones,' she said thoughtfully, standing up
and giving a wing salute. 'I am here to HELP.
Just tell me what you need . . .'

MOSS PIGLET

'We're on a really important mission, and we're running out of time,' said Marnie. Sharon was listening with every feather of her being. 'Someone very important is stuck on the moon, and someone else is about to destroy that moon!'

Sharon gasped. 'The moon? How?!'

'Earthworms and jetpacks,' Star answered.

'Never trust an earthworm with a jetpack,' sighed Sharon.

'But do you think, perhaps, you might be able to fly us to the moon?' Marnie asked.

Sharon bowed her head. 'It would be my HONOUR to serve you, tiny bug friends!' she said.

'We're forgetting one very important thing,' said Floyd. 'Can we actually survive in space?'

'I took Terry the Tyrant Tardigrade into space

once,' said Sharon. 'He said as long as I wear a helmet of sorts, I have forty-five per cent less chance of imploding.'

The colour drained from Floyd's stripes. 'Well, that's OK then . . .' he said sarcastically. 'And what did you say he was? A tar . . . di . . . grade?!'

'I've heard of tardigrades. They're even mini-er than minibeasts,' said Marnie. 'More like MICRO-beasts! Sometimes they're called water bears because they're super cute and squidgy.'

'Terry the Tyrant preferred to be called a moss piglet,' said Sharon.

Floyd sighed. 'I'm not sure I feel comfortable taking advice from someone called that.'

'I don't usually trust someone with the name Terry either, but I can assure you he was a very genuine chap,' said Sharon. 'Made me a glorious bolognese the day before I took him into space.'

Sharon wriggled her feathery bottom as she poised herself at the edge of the museum roof.

'Hop on! And hold tight!' she shouted, bouncing from one leg to the other as she revved herself up in preparation for flight.

Sporting helmets made from old fairy lights Sharon had found amongst other junk in the attic, Marnie, Floyd and Star took their places on Sharon's feathery back.

'Commencing flight to the moon in THREE, TWO, ONE, AND –'

WHOOOOOOOOOOOSH!

They were off!

Sharon leaped from the edge of the roof, beating her wings. Floyd was busy screaming, while Marnie watched her tiny world grow even tinier beneath them. Many marvellous and perfectly preserved trees of all types dotted around the museum gardens in between the neatly cut baffleberry bush hedges and the main building.

Before long, the moth, the bee-who-was-an-A and the ant were so high in the night sky that it was hard to see the landscape below. The lights from all the buildings below began to blur, and you'd never have known that Miniopolis even existed!

Marnie breathed in the chilly night air and gazed upon the light of the moon above them as the wind bustled through her fluffy antennae. She felt ALIVE! There was no way she or her friends could have flown this high and this fast by themselves. Marnie was fascinated by the way Sharon's wings flapped as silently as a whisper, taking the friends higher and higher with seemingly no effort.

'You OK, kids?' Sharon called.

'My body is still here but I cannot account for my soul,' cried Floyd, holding on to Marnie's wings as tight as he could.

Sharon chuckled. 'I'm not sure why you're making such a fuss when you're a minibeast that can fly?'

'Unless . . .' said Star, raising an eyebrow. 'Are you . . . scared of heights?'

Floyd sighed. 'I've never been FOND of heights,' he admitted. 'Please don't tell anyone – it's a bit embarrassing!'

'No, it's not,' Marnie said gently. 'Anyway, we're all scared of something. I'm actually a bit scared of the dark.'

'Really?' Floyd and Star echoed in surprise.

'The moon has always helped me feel braver,' Marnie continued with a smile.

'I bet Star isn't scared of anything,' said Floyd, laughing.

Star gave a little shrug. 'Of course not.'

Sharon beat her wings harder, flying higher still. They were SO high that Marnie could have sworn the horizon began to curve! And the moon DEFINITELY looked bigger. They were getting closer now . . .

Marnie felt excitement and nerves fill her whole body. Would they really find Lunora on the moon?

A strong gust almost sent Marnie flying backwards as Sharon flapped her wings faster, but the little moth held on with all her might. Floyd hugged Marnie tight just behind, and Star braced herself at the back, handling the speedy and bumpy ride rather well as they flew higher beyond the stratosphere.

Marnie looked back towards Earth to see colourful wisps of green and pink dancing across its surface as the little bugs and the robin made their way into space!

Even though Marnie had always believed moon magic was real, she would never have believed she'd be flying into space on the back of a robin called Sharon, and that Lunora was still ALIVE! And never ever, in ten million, one hundred and eighty buzzillion years could Marnie have imagined going to the one place she'd always dreamed of.

The moon.

CHAPTER 19

ONE SMALL FLUTTER

'How will we find Lunora in time? The moon really IS huge!' said Floyd as they flew closer.

Marnie bit her lip. To be honest, now she was here, she wasn't sure how they would find Lunora either!

Just then Marnie felt the tips of her antennae tingle all the way through to her wings. Everything went blurry around her, then she heard Lunora's voice in her mind. The voice whispered, 'Sea of Tranquillity.'

Marnie gasped. 'Sea of Tranquillity!' she bellowed.

Her vision sharpened and she turned to see Floyd and Star's VERY confused faces.

'Are you OK, Marnie?' asked Floyd. 'You're saying strange words . . .'

'I just heard Lunora's voice,' breathed Marnie. 'She's using moon magic to tell me that she's at the Sea of Tranquillity.'

'The sea? The moon has oceans?' shrieked Floyd as they flew over large, dark patches below them.

'No, no, there's no actual water on the moon.' Marnie laughed. 'I remember reading about this. Years and years ago, minibeasts used to think that the dark patches were oceans, but when the very first moths landed on the moon, they discovered the patches were actually huge areas of solidified lava! The Sea of Tranquillity is where the first moths landed, and now WE are about to follow in their flutterings!' She wriggled with joy and said, 'Sharon, I'll guide you! I know exactly where we need to go! Head north-east. The Sea of Tranquillity is a slightly bluey shade compared to the rest of the moon.'

'You sure know a lot about this place,' Sharon said, chuckling.

'I've read a lot of books,' said Marnie. 'And I have Lunora to thank, really. She's the one who inspired me . . . THERE!' she suddenly gasped, pointing to a large basin.

Sharon took a nosedive at super speed.

Floyd, for once, wasn't screaming . . . Mostly because he'd fainted in Star's arms.

Sharon spread out her wings as the moon's surface approached, slowing herself dramatically before touching down.

Marnie gazed around. She couldn't quite believe it . . . They were on the MOON!

The ground looked as if it were made of silvery sparkly dust, and everything was so . . . peaceful. Marnie could have spent hours and hours watching the stars twinkling in the vast space around them. Being here felt as natural as the antennae on her head.

'One small flutter for a moth . . .' she said to herself.

'. . . one giant flutter for moth-kind,' said a voice behind her.

Marnie turned to see an elderly moth walking slowly across the silvery Sea of Tranquillity. It was her ultimate hero . . . Lunora Wingheart!

And she was clutching a large book under one of her arms.

Marnie couldn't speak.

Lunora laughed. 'You look as if you've seen a ghost!'

'I . . . I . . .' Marnie stammered. 'I feel like I have . . .'

'Is that –' Floyd spluttered as he blinked his eyes open. Then he fainted again.

Star marched up to Lunora and shook one of her hands.

'We're very glad you're not dead,' she said. 'I'm Star, that's Floyd and this is Sharon. And here is Marnie, your biggest fan.'

Marnie stepped a little closer to Lunora.

'Is it really you?' she said. 'You're THE Lunora Wingheart?'

'Last time I checked!' Lunora said, chuckling as she patted herself down. 'Well, mostly . . .' She lifted one of her wings to reveal a large rip and smiled sadly. 'My flying days are over,' she said. 'I got injured on the way here all those years ago and couldn't fly back home.'

Marnie was still in utter disbelief at the whole situation. Then she frowned. 'You've been up here all alone for so long . . .'

'I've not really been alone,' said Lunora. 'You've all been keeping me company.'

She pointed behind Marnie. As the little moth turned, she saw Planet Earth looking more beautiful than ever.

'I hadn't truly appreciated just how spectacular our planet was until I saw it from our moon's point of view . . .' said Lunora. 'You'd never know that, right at this very moment, Earth is packed full to the brim with minibeasts. It's our home. The only home we've ever known – home to everyone, and everything.'

Marnie couldn't stop smiling. It truly was a wondrous sight.

'Plus, *this* has kept me very busy . . .' From beneath her tattered wing, Lunora pulled out the large book she'd been holding, embossed with silvery writing.

Marnie gasped. 'Is that . . .'

Lunora smiled and nodded. 'The Book of Moon Spells.'

CHAPTER 20

TOO BURLY TO DIE

'I always believed in moon magic,' said Lunora, 'but when I found the Book of Moon Spells here, just as the critter tales told, I knew for sure moon magic was real.'

She passed the book over to Marnie, who thought she might implode with happiness. Marnie touched the cover lightly. It was real. It was REALLY real!

She opened it. The pages were packed with curly scrawls and strange diagrams, drawn by the moths of centuries past. There were notes on how to read the stars and the phases of the moon – and all sorts of magical spells: from invisibility, super speed and transformation, to healing, super scent and bioluminescence. Marnie noticed that each spell had a tiny picture of the moon next to it.

'What does this mean?' she asked Lunora.

'When you're casting the spell from Earth, that particular spell will only work when the moon is in that specific phase,' Lunora explained. 'But I've been able to use all the spells since I have been ON the moon. For years I've been practising them. It's not easy, but with the communication spell I was able to connect to another moth from far away. I tried to connect to my brother, but

he kept shutting me out. When I connected with you, I knew right away you were special. Your belief in moon magic made the connection easier. I hope I didn't scare you.'

'Not at all!' said Marnie. 'I thought I was just having dreams at first, or that my imagination was running wild. But every time it happened, I couldn't help feeling like there was something more going on.'

She pored over the pages, wanting to read every single word and study every single picture. She was so overwhelmed with wonder that she almost forgot where she was and WHY she was there. Marnie snapped back to reality and closed the book.

'The worms!' she cried. 'They're going to destroy the moon!'

Lunora looked baffled. 'Excuse me? Worms? Destroying the moon?! How? When?'

'Now!' cried Marnie. 'Our schoolteacher set up a group of the best earthworm burrowers to fly here on pollen-powered jetpacks and burrow their way through the moon. I think they want to destroy it!'

'Why would your teacher want to do that?' gasped Lunora.

'He really hates the moon,' said Star.

There was a rumbling sound. The ground began to vibrate, almost knocking Marnie and her friends over.

'What on earthworm is happening?!' Floyd squeaked.

'I think exactly THAT,' Marnie shouted over the noise. 'EARTHWORMS!'

One by one, row upon row of very large
earthworms wearing jetpacks popped out of
the moon's surface, sending silvery plumes of
moondust into the air.

The earthworms froze mid-burrow as they
caught sight of Sharon, their eyes as wide as the
moon itself!

There was a moment of shocked silence before
one of the worms screamed: 'THE EEEARLY
BIIIIIRD IS HERE!'

Then it was chaos.

'I'M TOO BURLY TO DIIIIIIIE!'

'I STILL HAVE SO MUCH TO LIVE FOR!'

'I HAVEN'T SEEN THE LAST EPISODE OF *THE ANTS GO MARCHING*!'

They began burrowing back into their holes: a mass of wriggly tails and abs.

'STOP!' Sharon bellowed.

That seemed to work.

'You had better stop ruining the moon THIS INSTANT, or else . . .' She paused for a moment. 'I'll GOBBLE UP THE LOT OF YA!' She gave Marnie a secret wink, looking ever so proud of herself.

The earthworms huddled together, shuddering with fright.

Sharon hopped forward. 'Which one of you is Mr Atlas?' she said. 'Because you, sir, are in BIG trouble.'

The earthworms parted to reveal the teacher, wearing his own jetpack and helmet. Mr Atlas seemed to be frozen to the spot, his antennae bolt upright.

Sharon peered at him, bringing her face close to his. At the same time, Marnie appeared at her side, followed by Floyd and Star.

The teacher's expression darkened. He glared at Marnie. 'YOU!' he spat.

Lunora joined the gang and it was then that Mr Atlas's face completely transformed.

Lunora's eyes grew wide before she croaked, 'Brother?'

CHAPTER 21

WINSTON

'WHAT?' Marnie, Floyd, Star and Sharon all gasped in unison.

'Did she say brother?!' squeaked Marnie.

Lunora was staring at Mr Atlas.

The teacher's antennae drooped and he fell to his knees. 'It can't be . . .' he whispered. 'I . . . I thought you were dead!'

The two moths embraced each other.

'Winston, my dear little brother – I've missed you so much!' cried Lunora.

'I did not picture Mr Atlas being a Winston . . .' Floyd whispered. 'Definitely more of a Walt.'

'Oh, Lunora, I thought you'd been eaten by the Early Bird!' exclaimed Mr Atlas.

Sharon stepped forward and lifted a wing. 'No need to worry – I'm allergic to dairy.'

Mr Atlas took a wary step backwards.

'It's OK – she won't hurt you. This is Sharon, our friend,' said Marnie reassuringly. 'And without Sharon's help, we'd never have found Lunora.'

'Sorry to interrupt,' said one of the earthworms, peeping out from a hole in the ground. 'But do you still need us to burrow into the moon?'

Marnie recognised the mega worm. It was Alberto Gubble, aka the Absolute Unit.

'It's just that I haven't had dinner yet and, well, I'm starving . . .' he said.

Lunora folded her arms. 'You have some explaining to do, brother!' she said crossly. 'What's this I hear about you trying to destroy the magical moon? That's not the Winston I remember! You loved the moon, just like me! And why are you covering up your beautiful wings?'

Mr Atlas blinked back the tears in his big

yellow eyes, before slowly removing his cape
to reveal two large turquoise-coloured wings
decorated with moon patterns – just like
Lunora's.

'Why didn't you ever say that Lunora was your
sister?' asked Marnie.

Mr Atlas sighed and looked at the curious little
moth. This time there wasn't one ounce of hatred
in his expression. His eyes were filled with
sorrow.

'Lunora was always so passionate about the
moon and the idea of its magic. Same as you,
Marnie,' he said. 'I loved learning about the
moon, but I never believed in the magic. I felt
so guilty for not joining my sister on her special
trip to the moon.' He bowed his head. 'When she
never came home, I began to hate everything
about the moon . . . All it did was remind me of
Lunora, and what I'd lost.'

'Ah, this explains A LOT,' said Floyd.

'I was still a student at Minibeast Academy when she disappeared,' Mr Atlas continued. 'So when I became a teacher, I refused to teach *anything* about the moon.'

Mr Atlas turned to Marnie. 'From the moment we met, you reminded me so much of my sister,' he said.

Then, for the first time, he smiled – a genuine smile that lit up his whole face. And for the first

time Marnie could see just how much he looked like Lunora.

'I couldn't bear the thought of another young moth meeting the same fate as Lunora,' said Mr Atlas. 'Well . . . what I thought had happened to Lunora at the time.'

'So, in a really odd way, you were trying to protect Marnie?' asked Floyd.

The teacher looked taken aback by this comment, but chuckled. 'I guess that's one way of looking at it.' His gaze met Marnie's and he said gently, 'I'm sorry.'

Marnie had never thought she'd ever feel any sympathy towards Mr Atlas. He'd always been so mean, even before she knew about his terrible moon plan! But now she understood what had made him behave in that way.

'You've nothing to be sorry for,' Marnie said. 'I can't imagine life without my little brother Milo. If I were you, I'd have been angry with the moon too. My mum always told me that sometimes bugs can do silly things they wouldn't usually do when love is involved . . .' She raised an eyebrow. 'Even something REALLY silly like destroying the moon!'

Everyone was quiet for a moment, then they all burst out laughing.

Lunora and her brother hugged each other tightly.

'If it wasn't for the moon, we'd never have been reunited,' said Lunora. 'I was able to master the spell of communication to speak to Marnie. It took a very long time!'

'I kept thinking I was moondreaming about you,' said Marnie. 'Until I realised you really were talking to me!'

'Wait a minute,' said Mr Atlas, facing his sister. 'I also kept having dreams about you speaking to me . . . They were real?!'

Lunora nodded and chuckled.

'I'm so sorry,' said her brother. 'It broke my heart to keep seeing you in my dreams like that. So I avoided sleeping as much as possible . . . to avoid the dreams.'

THAT explains why he always looked so tired! thought Marnie.

'Oh, brother,' Lunora whispered sincerely, taking Mr Atlas's hand. 'There will be a day when one of us is here, but the other is not. Erasing everything that reminds us of each other will not help to heal you or make you feel happier. We must use all the things we love in life to help us to remember our happy times.'

'You're right, sister. You always were,' said Mr Atlas. 'And you always believed in moon magic.'

Marnie stepped forward and tapped Mr Atlas lightly on the wing.

'Does this mean you'll let us talk about the moon without getting told off?' she asked with a cheeky glint in her eyes.

'I think we're going to have to do better than that,' the teacher replied. 'I think we'd better make use of that forbidden classroom again. And perhaps my sister can be the one to do just that.' This was met with a squeal of approval from Marnie.

Lunora ruffled Marnie's fluffy hair. 'I shall revive the Moon Club! Let's call it the New Moon Club, where we can learn ALL about the moon and its magic.'

'REALLY?!' Marnie gasped. She thought she might just explode with excitement. 'A NEW, New Moon Club?'

'I can't think of a better way to spend my time,' said Lunora. 'Sharing my knowledge with a new generation who believe in the true magic of the moon. But, most importantly, believe in themselves. Just like you, Marnie.'

Marnie hugged Lunora tight. 'I'm so happy

the two minibeasts came to a door. Marnie gasped. An old sign hanging on by a thread read:

MOON CLUB.

The light of the moon shone brightly down upon the Museum of Nature, creating shimmery ribbons of silvery light through the gaps in the roof of Sharon's attic, where the minibeasts decided to gather and rest for a while. Marnie was thankful not to have to wear a fairy light on her head any more!

The place was wriggling with the muscly earthworms who had taken up Sharon's offer of petal pie, while others spent their time losing at multiple arm-wrestle tournaments against Star, before Floyd gathered the troops for a rather aggressive game of Scarabble.

Marnie sat with Lunora and Mr Atlas, looking through the Book of Moon Spells.

'There are so many spells in here,' said Marnie in awe. 'I can't wait to learn them all!'

'I think I'd like to have a go at this moon

magic too,' said Mr Atlas. 'I'm sad that you can't fly any more, though.' He gently touched the large rip in Lunora's wing, but his sister smiled and took his hand.

'It's OK,' she said. 'Sharon has offered to be my loyal robin-ride.' She chuckled. 'She's also said I can live in the attic with her above the Museum of Nature. I never imagined I'd end up befriending a bird!'

'And I never imagined finding my sister again,' said Mr Atlas with a twinkle in his eye.

Marnie couldn't quite believe the change in him. Mr Atlas already seemed like a different moth. When Marnie saw the way he looked at his sister with so much adoration and love, she felt her little heart swell!

Leaving the siblings alone together to catch up properly, Marnie skipped over to join Floyd and the Scarabble gang.

'Electroencephalogram is NOT a real word,'

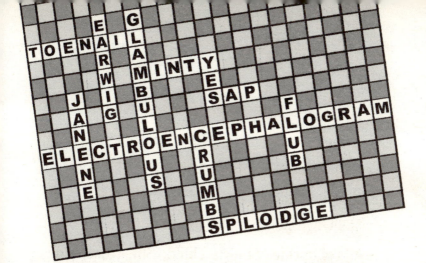

Floyd was saying crossly.

'It's the device used to measure electrical activity in the brain, so yes, it IS a real word,' said Star. 'But I think you'll find that glambulous is not.'

'It describes someone glamorous and fabulous,' Floyd argued. 'Like ME.'

'Well, you're being be ridiculous,' said Star.

'Oooh, I think I have the word flub,' Alberto Gubble added, merrily placing his letters on the board.

'Star's being a FLUB,' said Floyd.

'I'll FLUB you right in the stinger in a minute!' growled Star.

She glared at Floyd for a few moments before bursting out laughing. Marnie wasn't sure she'd ever seen Star look so relaxed and happy before. Then, to Marnie's complete surprise, Star took Floyd's hands and hers.

'Thank you,' the little ant said sincerely. 'Earlier on . . . when I said wasn't scared of anything,' she continued, shifting from side to side on the spot, 'that's not true.' She took a deep breath. 'Before knowing you, I didn't have any friends. Being a princess of an aggressive ant colony means it's all marching practice, being super tough, and some light conquering at the weekends. There was no option to be scared of anything. But now I have two of the best friends I could have ever hoped for. And, um, I am scared of losing you.'

Floyd's eyes welled up. 'Star Vonstrosity, I did not expect YOU to tug at my heart strings!' he said, clutching his pearls.

'Do not speak a word of it again,' Star said

darkly. 'Or I'll pluck your heart strings right out.'

'Noted!' Floyd saluted, before the three friends burst into fits of giggles and had a group hug.

Floyd used this opportunity to subtly add the word glambulous to the Scarabble board while Star wasn't looking.

Once everybody else had fallen asleep, Marnie, Floyd and Star sat on the eastern side of the roof of the museum to watch the sunrise.

'Do you think As and bees might be able to join the New Moon Club?' asked Floyd.

'Anyone can join the club!' said Marnie.

'Even ants?' asked Star hopefully.

The little moth grinned. 'The moon is there for us ALL to share, no matter how big or small you are. Maybe even Veronica and her friends will want to learn about it now!'

'Look,' said Floyd, pointing up at a cluster of stars. 'I think I've found the constellation of Floyd!' He pointed towards a group of stars that looked like the letter A.

'And I've found the constellation of Star . . .' said the little ant. 'Right there, and there and there and there . . . aaaand there!'

She pointed all over the star-speckled sky and

the friends found themselves rolling around laughing once again.

Marnie watched as the sky slowly turned from the dark of night, prickled with stars, to an inky purple tinged with deep orange, as the first rays of sunlight peeped through. But still visible in the sky was the moon, beginning its descent.

'So now we know that moon magic is real,' Floyd began with an excitable buzz, 'this could mean the story of Incy Wincy Spider climbing up the waterspout is indeed true! You've inspired me, Marnie, and I shall make it my mission to find out. After all, I am very nosy!'

Marnie chuckled and looked upon the museum gardens stretching before them, as the shadows changed shapes in the morning sunlight.

'Who'd have thought minibeasts as tiny as us would make it all the way to the moon,' Floyd added dreamily.

'Well, we might be small,' said Marnie, putting her wings around her best friends. 'But that'll never stop us from having BIG dreams!'

MAGNIFICENT MINIBEAST FACT AND FICTION!

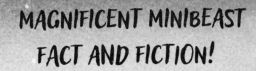

Marnie Midnight books take lots of inspiration from the natural world, but the critter characters do share some similarities with real-life creatures!

The real-life bugs you find in your garden would not be able to survive in space, even if they wore fairy-light helmets. But Tardigrades can survive in space and they really are referred to as Moss Piglets or Water Bears.

As far as we know, it is not possible for a bee to be part ladybird, but then Floyd is a total original!

Most names of the flowers and plants in the book are made up (unless you've ever spotted a naughty nigel or a step-dad's work week?!) but the shepherd's *purse* IS a real plant.

Worms do not have abs. (As far as we know!)

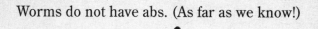

A bees' waggle dance IS real, but Floyd's version is unique to Marnie's world. (The real waggle dance is actually far more sophisticated, but don't tell Floyd!)

Ant colonies do go to war over territory or food, and they have some very aggressive battle techniques.

Ladybirds' spots may not be perfect circles, but they aren't square.

The wonderful moon can be used to navigate. Celestial navigation uses the moon, sun and stars to help work out where you are.

The Sea of Tranquillity is where the first human on the moon, Neil Armstrong, landed.

MARNIE MIDNIGHT

Look out for the next magical book in the series, coming soon!